I0616456

Learning from ISAAC

TARNISHED SOULS

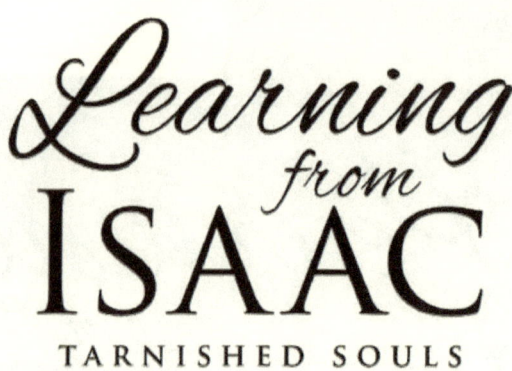

Learning *from* ISAAC

TARNISHED SOULS

DEV BENTHAM

www.DevBentham.com

Cover by Jordan Castillo Price

Edited by Jordan Castillo Price and Laurie Cheeley

An earlier version of this story was published by
Loose Id in 2012

Loose Id version edited by Larke Butler

Copyright 2012 Dev Bentham
ISBN 978-0-9832033-8-4

Warning sexual content: This book contains graphic imagery of men having sex together. And enjoying it. However, the story is primarily a romance. Don't be disappointed if you read pages and pages and pages without encountering acts, organs or orgasms.

Published by Love is a Light Press
POB 685, Minocqua, WI 54548

Acknowledgments

The Tarnished Souls series began with *Learning from Isaac* in more ways than one. When I first wrote the story, I had no plans for a romance series centering on Jewish holidays. The germ of that idea came when Loose Id picked up on the Passover dinner that forms a turning point in Nathan and Isaac's relationship and decided to launch the book during Passover. I loved the connection between what happens for both men in the story and the central Passover story of freedom from bondage. From there the idea of taking Jewish holiday themes and weaving them into a series of m/m romance stories was born.

This was only my second m/m romance. In the two years since its first release, I've completed three more Tarnished Souls stories and another three unrelated m/m romances, and I've learned a lot. While I had wonderful editing help from Larke Butler on the first release, my feeling was that readers hadn't connected with Nathan in the way I'd hoped. When it came time to rerelease the story, I decided on a significant rewrite. Since then, the story has grown (it's about 5% longer), there are a few minor plot changes, and I hope that both Nathan and Isaac are more fully portrayed. If you read the original, I think you'll find this an improved version. If this is the first time you've encountered these men, I hope you fall in love with them the way I did.

This story has benefitted greatly from the editorial suggestions of Larke Butler and the entire Loose Id team on the original version and the incomparable Jordan Castillo Price on this author release edition. Thanks also to Laurie Cheeley for her wonderful input into the story and amazing copyediting skills. The beautiful new cover is by Jordan Castillo Price.

Chapter One

I wrote on the board, *The first rule of ecology is that small shifts beget big change.*

Under that I added, *Everything is connected.*

Communicating my love of science to students was the best part of my job. I love interacting with all those fresh minds eager to change the world. But I hated the awkwardness of the first day of class. When I first started teaching, I was about five years older than most of my students. I felt connected to them—we were the same generation. But each year the students seemed to get younger. Fifteen years later that feeling of connection didn't happen on the first day, or even in the first week. With most of the students, I still got there eventually, but every year it took more work.

Isaac sat in the back row, third seat from the window. Sunlight streamed through the glass forming a golden finger that landed like a caress on his chiseled cheekk. Most of the other students I recognized, having passed them in the hallway from time to time as they stumbled through their first years here. Many of my colleagues developed close relationships with the students, watching them grow through four, and sometimes five, years of the expensive education their parents were providing. I, on the other hand, only had them in one course, a class sufficiently physically and intellectually grueling that I was sure they were grateful that one course was all they had to take from me. But I did take note of them as they passed my office in small, chatty clusters or single, preoccupied strolls.

And I certainly would have noticed Isaac with his dark curls and elegant stride, so different from the beefy men and outdoorsy women who normally peopled my world. Students at Saint Genevieve's, a small Catholic college in the suburbs of Chicago, tended to clomp around campus in ragged jeans and thick, plaid wool shirts. Among these dandelions, Isaac, with his tight dark jeans, long-sleeved tees, and strong Jewish profile, stuck out like a lily. My first thought on seeing him was, wouldn't my mama be proud if I brought home such a nice Jewish boy? My second was, are you out of your frigging mind?

I was neither out nor in at school, simply a single, perpetual bachelor academic. I'd let it be known that my previous relationships did not pan out, mostly because of work. My colleagues understood. Their own marriages and entanglements suffered from the seventy-hour workload we shouldered each week in order to teach and research the subjects about which we were most passionate. It might not have surprised most of them, and I wouldn't have lost my job, if I let it be known that the person who moved out a few years ago was named Bill. Jenny Karn, our marvelous microbiologist, brought Leslie with her to all department functions. But I did know, very well, the passage in the morals clause I signed, the one that related to schtupping students. It was grounds for dismissal, no matter their gender.

And so I looked at everyone but Isaac Wolf as I lectured that fine September morning. But I can't remember anyone else who was there.

* * * *

I dismissed the students with only minutes to go before the Friday faculty meeting. Our chair, a chemist named Geoffrey Dunn, insisted that four on Friday was the only time when everyone was free to meet. Never mind that Wednesdays at eight in the morning were equally free, that several faculty members had children who needed to be picked up from school or day care in the late afternoon, or that by late Friday everyone was in a foul mood. The time suited Geoffrey.

I sprinted across campus to the library. We met in a conference room buried in the bowels of the old rambling building. I padded through the stacks, passing students already engaged in research—or cruising each other amidst the books. The conference room door was closed, meaning Geoffrey had started without me. No surprise. I wasn't one of his favorite colleagues. I could never tell if it was some sort of unconscious homophobia or that I challenged him whenever he was spectacularly wrong. Or maybe he simply didn't like me.

I didn't like him either. Geoffrey wanted to destroy my course—the only class I taught, a yearlong survey of ecological sampling techniques that was required for students in the natural resources program. Saint Genevieve's had a surprisingly good history of placing students in the few natural resources jobs available to undergraduates and an astonishingly high rate of acceptance for graduate programs in the field. I liked to think it was because of my course. Years later I heard from students that mine was the course that changed their lives.

That was what kept me teaching.

Geoffrey Dunn and his faculty meetings were not. I anticipated his glare as I opened the door.

Geoffrey chose to ignore me as I slipped into the vacant chair beside Jenny. She smiled and passed me an agenda. I skimmed the contents.

"Are we going to battle this crap again?" I muttered under my breath to her, pointing to the fifth item on the agenda.

She gave me a sympathetic glance.

For five years running, Geoffrey had proposed we change the requirements for the major. He had a few scattered suggestions here and there, but the big one was to turn my sixteen-credit methods course into an elective, which would cut its enrollment in half. The inevitable result would be that the course would shift to an every-other-year schedule, and I'd be left to teach everyone else's leftovers on the off years. Not to mention that half our graduates would be flung into the world with no practical skills.

I was tired of the debate and could have argued both sides in my sleep. Geoffrey would contend that my course was too hard, that I drove students away from the program and kept them from taking other courses, most notably his own favorite, which was periodically canceled due to low enrollment. I would argue that while students came into my course seeing it as a grade point killer, by the end of the year most of them were happy with the marketable skills they'd learned. It was the last chance students got to learn techniques they'd need for a career in natural resource management. Sure, I demanded a lot. Our fragile planet's future was in their sweaty palms. Sometimes that scared me to death. Sometimes it made me hopeful.

So far my colleagues had agreed with me. At some point the politics might shift toward him. I wasn't sure what I'd do then. Resign in a fit of pique or meekly acquiesce to teach whatever crumbs he gave me? Whichever way the wind was going to blow, I wasn't up to the debate this early in the year, and let a few other faculty argue in favor of keeping my course. Geoffrey and his cronies said their predictable bits, and eventually the question was tabled and the meeting droned on. My course had survived another meeting.

After adjournment, I turned to Jenny as she gathered her belongings. "Hey, do you know a student named Isaac Wolf? He's in my capstone class."

Her face split into a wide smile. "Isaac? He's a great kid. Really smart. You'll like having him in class."

I scraped back my chair, getting ready to stand. "I don't think I've seen him around before."

She stood. "He took a couple of years off. He stopped by my office last week. I'm not surprised you didn't recognize him. He's grown out his hair and gotten rid of the glasses. Slimmed down some too."

I nodded. "That would explain it."

"How's the research going?" Jenny asked as we made our way out of the room.

"Very well, actually. I signed three new clients over the summer. We should have plenty to do this winter." In addition to my own work on Bioindicators—the aquatic organisms who act as canaries in the coal mines for polluted waterways—I ran a small business identifying worms and insects sent to me by state agencies and other researchers interested in quantifying the extent of impact a given pollution event has had on their water body. The funds generated supported student workers and bought necessary equipment, and I got a great deal of personal satisfaction from the work. None of which eased the essential loneliness of my life. But it helped pass the time.

* * * *

I hated the Friday faculty meetings, but, invariably, halfway home I'd be wishing I was still there. It had been almost three years, but ever since Bill left, the apartment, already small, seemed to cave in on me. I didn't pretend we'd had a good relationship and I probably should have felt relief when he went. Instead I was angry. I'd put up with a lot—his jokes about how dry and boring I was, his drinking, the other men and watching the clock tick by on a Saturday night wondering if he would decide to come home. What had I gotten in return? A burning urethra, ten days of antibiotics, and a bone deep fear that lasted for months while I had myself tested and tested and re-tested until I could be sure I was clean.

Now I was over him. The air no longer vibrated with my unresolved anger. But I had once thought I'd loved Bill and I still missed having someone I could care about more than I cared about work or the state of the world or even myself. Alone, all those things filled the apartment until it was hard to breathe. I stayed away as much as possible, eating in restaurants, visiting my mother, grading in coffee shops, working in my lab until I was tired enough to fall asleep without dreaming. I couldn't wait to be back in the classroom on Monday.

* * * *

One Monday, Isaac looked up at me from under those impossibly long lashes, his smile slow and sexy, as I dropped the nearly perfect, graded midterm on his desk. The night before I'd added *brilliant* to the growing list of adjectives strung in my head beside his name. Which didn't help. Smart was sexy. And in the morning, I'd woken from a dream so vivid I was surprised to find myself alone. My lips tingled with the fantasy of his beautiful collarbone beneath them. Now I looked down at that same spot peeking from beneath his unbuttoned stark white shirt. For a moment I stood mesmerized by his cider-colored skin against the white.

My eyes met his for an instant. Every year at least a couple of the young women flirted with me, usually shyly, but occasionally more overtly. Once before I'd had a male student awkwardly express his interest. But this was different. Every cell in my body was on high alert. Isaac's half smile and the hot brown light of his eyes let me know I'd been discovered. He knew I wanted him. The shift in power between teacher and student was palpable.

I gave the briefest of nods. "Well done, Mr. Wolf."

Isaac's smile widened. "Thank you, Dr. Kohn."

His smile and the promise it contained followed me around the room as I delivered the bad news of the first graded test. It left my heart pounding, whether from terror or anticipation, I couldn't tell.

Chapter Two

Theoretical understanding only goes so far. Each year on a chilly Monday morning in early November, after two months in the classroom, I load the students into a bus and take them for five days to a field station up north. In good years, the sun dapples our path through the trees, and we eat lunch on the pier, wearing fleece and long underwear. But most years we're slogging through rain and snow, our feet and hands aching with cold. I've thought about moving the week up into September, when we might expect better weather, but it doesn't fit the curriculum. Besides, those few who will actually enter the profession need to be tough.

A light snow was falling at seven a.m. when the students arrived in the school parking lot. They laughed and joked, bundled in their down parkas, carrying well-used outdoor gear. Isaac appeared, somehow looking cool and collected in an ancient canvas coat and old-man galoshes, a worn duffel slung over one shoulder. I would later find out he'd spent a week scouring thrift stores, but at the moment I saw him, he looked like a hip version of a peddler from our shared ancestral heritage. I wondered if six days and nights in close proximity would tarnish the gleam I felt every time I saw him.

The field trip was where my class coalesced. Whether by

the end of the year they loved or hated me, for the most part, they liked each other. After fifteen years, I could predict the moment when they melded into a single unit. The worse the weather, the quicker that moment came.

I drove north, ignoring the talk behind me. Occasionally my attention would be caught by the promise of gossip about my colleagues, but invariably it was nothing more exciting than who passed back papers or tests, or who graded too hard. After years of faculty meetings, I knew my colleagues far too well for any of that to be news. A small, petty part of me hoped to hear something damning about Geoffrey Dunn, but if there was dirt to dish, I didn't hear it that morning.

Every few miles, my eyes strayed to the rearview mirror. Isaac sat in a seat by himself, curled against the window asleep. Students at Saint Genevieve's are discouraged from taking jobs, but some work nights, and I wondered if he was one. Or maybe he'd been out partying with the boys. A gorgeous, self-assured young man like him wasn't likely to live the celibate existence of an over-forty academic. The thought of him tangled in sweaty sheets with another undergraduate was both exciting and disheartening. I turned my attention back to the road.

The college paid for us to stay a week in the only winterized building of a summer camp--a great, wooden, dining hall with thick-paned windows and an industrial kitchen, half of which we devoted to a field lab and the other half to cooking, most of which was done by committee. In the back of the cavernous dining room, we set up cots for men on one side of the room, for women on the other, with me a reluctant chaperone between. That first night I lay on my cot, listening to the creak of the old building and the breathing of twenty students, trying to distinguish Isaac's. To call the old, drafty dining hall heated was an exaggeration. The pipes might not have been freezing, but the tip of my nose peeking out from my sleeping bag was. I lay still and tried not to imagine Isaac on his cot, less than twenty feet away. From one side of the hall I heard a woman shuffle to the bathroom. Someone on the men's side slid out of their sleeping bag. I ignored them. The dining hall was too public for romance, but I suspected every year some quiet coupling went on in the other rooms or the woods outside. The university would have liked me to be more vigilant but the students were consenting adults. Who was I to police their romances? In my perfect world I'd have one of my own.

* * * *

Beginning on Thursday morning, the next to last day of our field trip, I always had the students participate in a twenty-four hour study of zooplankton migration within the nearby lake. The twenty-four hour study gave the students plenty of experience with the nets and traps we used to catch zooplankton, and provided samples that took us through a month of indoor labs, after which the data analysis was yet another test of their abilities.

The sampling itself was grueling, particularly for those unlucky enough to end up on a cold November night in a small boat in the middle of the lake. At the beginning of the week I posted a sheet. They could sign up in pairs for a two-hour slot, and first thing, I pencilled myself in to work with some unlucky, sleepy undergraduate from two to four in the morning. Since I was the one who made them stay up all night, it was only fair I took the worst shift. The right to sign up early and avoid the night hours was earned by good deeds, since students couldn't put their names down until they'd worked on both a cooking and a cleanup crew. Those quick to volunteer for kitchen duty ended up sampling zooplankton in the relative warmth of the afternoon. Those more reluctant to serve their classmates put their names to increasingly later spots. It was intimidating to spend two hours in a confined space with your professor, so invariably, the dotted line beneath my name was the last to fill.

Early Tuesday morning, I gathered the three students who had already met the requirement and handed them the pen and permission to sign themselves into any shift. The first two didn't surprise me. Sue Taylor, a nervous blonde woman with an annoying habit of snapping her gum, and her more laid-back friend, Jane Good, who wore her long brown hair in a ponytail covered by a Cubs ball cap, had both worked in my lab for two years. They were my most dependable and hardest working employees. I wasn't surprised to find they'd earned the right to sign up first. Together they scarfed up the prime spot, the daylight slot opposite mine. Jane passed the pen to Isaac with a lopsided grin. He nodded solemnly and glanced at me, his expression blank except for the glint of amusement in his eyes. My heart rate sped as I watched him quickly scrawl his name next to mine. He handed back my pen with a wink. My mouth went dry as he sauntered away.

* * * *

Thursday dawned cold and clear. I woke early and tiptoed in my stockinged feet to the kitchen to start the coffee. While it brewed, I stood at the window, staring out at the lake, hoping I could believe the weather reports that predicted more of the same throughout the day and into the night. In a small boat on a cold lake in the middle of the night, rain and snow can be punishing.

I heard footsteps behind me, and Isaac stood beside me, his gaze also out the window. The morning sun lit his soft curls like a dark halo. He smelled of toothpaste and musty sleeping bag. It was all I could do to stand rigid beside his wild beauty.

"Shouldn't you be sleeping?" I whispered. "We have a late night tonight."

He turned to me with a smile. "Could say the same to you."

The golden lights glowing from deep in his irises left me speechless. I tried to look away but found myself staring instead at the pink swell of his lower lip. His mouth opened, and I had a glimpse of teeth and tongue.

I drew breath, recalling myself. I had no business standing in a cold kitchen with hot thoughts about this young man, a student, who was little more than half my age. The pressure in my groin was entirely inappropriate. I turned and strode to the coffee urn.

With my back to him, I cleared my throat, determined to respond only to his words and not to the invitation in his eyes. "I want to make sure the first sampling shift goes well."

He sounded amused. "You worry too much."

"Perhaps." I poured coffee, the first sip hot enough to burn my tongue. "You can never be too careful."

I heard the clink of a coffee cup as he took one down from the cupboard. I looked up as he neared.

"But if you don't take chances, you never know what you're missing."

We clearly weren't talking about class anymore. I started to speak but stopped as the door swung open and a bleary-eyed Jane stumbled in. I stepped away from Isaac and left the kitchen, accompanied only by the pounding of my heart.

* * * *

I was already awake, staring into the dark when my watch beeped. In the bathroom I gazed into the wavy metal surface that served as a mirror. Rubbing my five-day growth of stubble, I regretted not bringing a razor. Usually I let myself go scruffy in an effort at humanizing my image with the students. I contemplated the dark mat of bristles, vaguely disturbed by the smattering of salt amid the pepper. In the last few years I'd almost convinced myself that the gray streaks at my temples conferred authority and made me look distinguished. It was harder to believe at one in the morning, in the bleak light of the camp bathroom, as I was about to spend a few hours in the company of a spectacularly attractive young man.

"Like what you see?" I jumped at the sound. Isaac seemed to have materialized out of nowhere.

"Not really." I twisted the faucets and splashed water on my face.

Isaac leaned a hip against the second sink and watched

me. "The beard's sexy. Gives you a rugged look."

I snorted into my towel as I dried my face. "I'll keep that in mind."

Isaac's shoulders lifted in an elegant shrug. His own face looked smooth. I wanted to reach out and run my hand across it. Obviously he'd not only brought a razor but used it at ought-nothing in the morning. That thought sent a shiver of excitement through me.

The air between us thickened. My cock thickened with possibility. Isaac leaned toward me. I cleared my throat and stepped back.

"I'll get us a thermos of coffee. You like it with cream?"

With a grin, Isaac let the inadvertent double entendre settle between us. His smile widened. "Yeah, bring some sugar packets too. I saved cookies from dinner. I'll get them and meet you down at the dock."

What on earth could he see in me? Students get crushes on teachers. And it's natural that sometimes those feelings are reciprocated. After all, our students are all adults. But the power difference between student and teacher made it ethically irresponsible for the teacher to engage. I'd also seen colleagues skate close to the line. Some probably crossed over. I'd never been tempted. Before now. I watched the door for a long moment after Isaac left, wondering how the hell I was going to resist him.

* * * *

Isaac and I stood together, watching the second most unlucky pair row toward the dock. Above us, the sky was littered with stars. The sliver of a waxing moon slipped toward the horizon. Waves slapped gently against the pilings. We could hear the dip and pull of oars through the water. My breath puffed out in little clouds in the white light of my headlamp.

"How'd it go?" I asked as the boat pulled near.

"Fucking cold," one of the dark bundles replied. It sounded like my most challenged student, a stoner who showed up late for class every day.

"I think we got everything, Professor Kohn." The other young man threw me the boat line. I recognized Thad Miller, one of my more solid B students. "Really freezes your hands after a while, though."

I gave them a hand getting out of the boat. "Better go in and get warm. I left a kettle boiling if you want to make some cocoa. Otherwise, please turn it off."

"Yes, sir," Thad called as they lugged their equipment and samples toward the cabin.

While I held the boat, Isaac hefted in our supplies, swung his leg over, and slid gracefully into the middle seat. I pushed us off and jumped in. Isaac took the oars and began rowing us toward the center of the little lake. With each stroke, he leaned forward and pitched back with ease. His oars hit the water silently, and the boat glided forward.

"You've rowed before." My voice sounded loud against the silent lake.

"Crew team freshman and sophomore years." It made sense. His strokes were clean and strong.

I settled back a little on my bench. "Not since?"

He shrugged mid-stroke. "I don't have time anymore."

I pulled out my GPS and listened to the sound of the water rushing by our boat as I watched the coordinates. There's a buoy at the sampling spot, but it can be hard to find in the dark. Between Isaac's strong arms and my navigation, we found it and tied off to the buoy. I set up the electric lantern, and we clicked off our headlamps.

The cold invaded my bones as I helped Isaac prepare the sampling gear. We worked together, silently at first, then I started on my standard student questions. "What are your plans after this year?"

He looked up at me, his hands pausing on the line. He gave one of those lovely shrugs. "I'm applying to graduate school for the fall, and hoping to get an internship with an environmental engineering firm this summer. Maybe something that could go permanent after I'm through school."

I rubbed my hands together, trying to warm them. "That's what you'd like to do eventually? Work in environmental engineering?"

He cocked his head. "You sound disapproving."

I shook my head. "No, not at all. It's only that most students in our program dream of fieldwork. Environmental engineering would be a stretch for your average Saint Genevieve grad. Where are you applying for graduate school?"

He pulled the trap out of the water, and we spent a few minutes filling and labeling bottles before he answered. "Here and there. My first choice is University of Wisconsin-

Madison, but I'll go wherever I can get a fellowship that will pay my way."

I helped heft the next piece of gear overboard. "Are you from Chicago?"

He shook his head. "New York. Brooklyn, actually. But I like the Midwest. It's more relaxed. You?"

I smiled. "Chicago born and bred. It's why I took the job here. I like being near my family."

A small shudder rippled through Isaac.

I reached for the thermos. "You're cold. And tired, I imagine. It's late."

Isaac shrugged but accepted the plastic coffee cup and sugar packets when I offered them. "I'm used to late nights from work."

"Where do you work?" I sipped the coffee, relishing the warmth that flowed in with it.

"A club downtown." He busied himself with sugar packets and coffee stirring.

I smiled at him. "Should I give you my standard speech about how you can't possibly earn enough at a minimum-wage job to make up for the impact working will have on your grades?"

He shrugged again, and I let it drop. Isaac's grades weren't suffering, and it wasn't my concern if he wanted to make some spending money on the side.

I found myself contemplating his face in the diffuse florescence of the lantern. "What attracted you to this field?

There aren't many of us in the environmental sciences."

He glanced at me. "Gays?"

I blinked at him, realizing that in fifteen years I had never come out to a student. "That, too. But I was thinking of Jews."

He smiled. Clearly, his question had been a fishing expedition, and I'd been caught. With a grin, he proceeded to argue the Jewish point, listing environmental scientists with Jewish names.

I laughed and held up my hands in a gesture of surrender. "You win."

He looked at me from under his long, dark lashes, his expression a little uncertain. "You are, though, right?"

"Jewish?"

In the dim light it was hard to tell, but it looked like he blushed. "Gay."

I nodded briefly as I closed my eyes and inhaled the cold, clean smell of pine and lake. When I opened them again, he was watching me. I looked away.

The boat rocked as he moved. I gasped as I felt his weight on my legs. He ran his hands up the inside of my thighs until his face was inches from mine. I thought he was going to kiss me. My brain screamed that I had to stop him. I leaned forward.

Isaac sat back. "Just so you know."

I took a deep breath and tried to focus. My thighs still tingled and my thoughts wouldn't come together. Finally I gestured toward the sampling gear. Isaac smiled and began to haul it up, peering into the black water to make sure the line stayed straight.

Once my pulse slowed, I spoke quietly, wanting to get it all out before he touched me again and I lost my will. "I was worried that being gay would be a problem when I first came to Saint Genevieve's and had a confidential chat with one of the priests. He told me my sexual orientation wouldn't be an issue unless I chose to inflict it on a student. He pointed out that the church was now sensitized to that kind of exploitation and that examples would be made."

Isaac stopped pulling the trap up and stared at me. "Inflict? Exploit? You mean because of the pedophile priests? But those were children. I'm not—"

I held up my hand to stop him. "Isaac, I can't."

He turned back to the trap and pulled it slowly through the water and into the boat. When our samples were filled, he looked at me again. "But would you want to, if I weren't a student?"

With every cell of my being. I could hear my own heartbeat. He would have been able to tell for himself how much I wanted him if it hadn't been for the dim light, the fall of my jacket, and the looseness of my pants.

I took a deep breath. "If I tell you the truth, it will only get us in deeper trouble."

He leaned forward and rested his hands on my knees again. Even through his gloves, my rough trousers, and a layer of long underwear, his touch was electrifying. "No, it won't. I promise. Either way, I'll back off."

I took off my glove and reached out to touch a curl that sprang from beneath his cap. For a moment, I let my gaze roam his face, let him see the hunger. My fingers trailed down his smooth jaw. His eyes remained locked on mine. I dropped my hand and put back on my glove. "I already want to. If you weren't a student, I would."

He sat up. "I won't always be your student."

Talk like that could make my heart ache. "We can see about that when and if the time comes. But you're likely to find someone in the meantime. Someone younger."

He smiled slowly. "Maybe."

We worked in silence for another hour. When our time was up, Isaac rowed us back to the dock, where another pair of students awaited.

"You go on up," I told Isaac as we approached. "I'll help get these guys going."

He winked. "Yeah, I've got something to take care of, myself. And I'll be thinking of you."

I closed my eyes, unwilling to admit my own plans to find somewhere private to fantasize as soon as the boat was launched. "You promised," I whispered.

"I know." His voice was warm and soft, barely carrying through the cold night air. "Think of it as a parting shot."

I opened my eyes and gave him a sad smile. I turned to greet our replacements as they called their hellos.

Chapter Three

Back at school, Isaac was true to his word and kept his distance. The semester trudged on. I tried not to watch for him as I arrived on campus. I live close enough to bicycle to work, which reduces my carbon footprint and helps me get a little exercise. The route takes me past a few stores, the dorms, a pizza place, and a coffeehouse—all hangouts for Saint Genevieve students. While many waved or greeted me, Isaac was never among them.

Between work in my research lab and teaching, the remaining days until Thanksgiving break flew by. On the Wednesday before Thanksgiving I stood at my desk, chatting with students as they packed up to leave. The classroom had a festive air, spirits soaring with the prospect of four days off and a chance to sleep. Thad Miller politely asked what I was doing for Thanksgiving. I explained that for as long as I could remember, my mother and I had volunteered at a soup kitchen on Thanksgiving. As always, it was a showstopper, and the students murmured their approval. I smiled and allowed their new vision of me as an altruistic Samaritan to settle in without adding that I had thrown a tantrum every year as a child, and even deep into my twenties I'd only grudgingly accompanied my mother from her elegant neighborhood to the grubby institutional food distribution center for which she was a founding board member. I'd softened with age. These days it no longer felt like either a trial to endure or a mitzvah to perform, but rather simply what we did on the holiday.

I looked up to see Isaac on the fringe of the crowd.

"And what are you all doing?" I asked the circle of faces. They burbled about family and football. My gaze rested on Isaac's.

"Working," he muttered. "And going to a friend's for dinner tomorrow."

My stomach clenched at the words. Had he found someone this soon?

Sue Taylor appeared beside him. "I'm not sure he's ready for my crazy family. But my mom makes a great pumpkin pie."

Isaac smirked as I felt the color returning to my cheeks.

* * * *

Mom was in fine form that night. When I was a boy, I thought she was the most beautiful woman on earth. I don't know that I was wrong about that. At sixty-two, wide-hipped and quick-tongued, Becca Kohn was a force of nature.

She greeted me at the door. "You look pale. Are you getting enough sleep?"

"Yes, Mother." I kissed her cheek, dusting my lips with her expensive, sweet-smelling face powder.

In her dark suit and pearls, she looked every inch the successful defense attorney she was and not at all the radical reformer who stared back at me from the photos lining the front hallway. These photos of my parents—in some they posed with civil rights leaders, others captured them at a rally or march—were the only memories I had of my father. He was drafted into the army before I was born. The story was that my mother begged him to escape to Canada, but he wouldn't. A few months later, he left for Vietnam and was dead before we could meet. Mom named me after him. She didn't get married again, choosing instead to go back to school and transform herself into someone who would never again be a victim of someone else's choices. A few years ago she'd started dating Jeremiah Bridges, a widower with grown children of his own. He regularly asked her to marry him, and just as regularly, she turned him down.

"Where's Jeremiah?" I asked, following her into the hallway.

She shrugged. "At his daughter's in Atlanta."

"Why didn't you go with him? I'm sure Ruth would have loved to have you." I'd met Jeremiah's oldest daughter the previous summer. Ruth told me she was delighted he'd found someone to love. Mom said his other two children were less than pleased that their father was cavorting with a white woman.

She shook her head. "He has his traditions. We have ours. I'd offer you a glass of wine, but our reservations are for seven." She handed me her coat. I held it while she put it on. "You did drive, didn't you? We'll never get there in time on the bus."

My mother doesn't own a car. She sees them as a blight on the urban landscape. She is, however, happy to ride in mine on occasion and will even call me rather than a taxi when she needs to travel outside the proscribed circuits of the Chicago Transit Authority. Or when it's more convenient.

While customers clustered at a few tables, it was clear that a reservation hadn't been necessary at the Indian restaurant on Halsted that Mom had chosen for our pre-Thanksgiving feast. A waiter led us to a table for two near the window and produced papadum—crisp lentil crackers—along with its accompanying condiments. We perused our menus, discussed the possible choices, and ordered curries, dal, and naan.

As the waiter strode away, Mom rested her elbows on the table and looked at me. "Tell me how you really are, Nathan."

I shrugged. "The same. It's a good group this year, but nothing really changes."

She cracked off a piece of papadum and dipped it into the green mint sauce. "I ran into Kenny Marks' mother the other day. She said he'd be home for their big New Year's event this year."

I smiled. How many years had it been that Mom and Sarah Marks had been trying to fix us up? "You do know that Kenny's very happy with his boyfriend in LA, right? George is a very nice man. Remember, you met him at the Marks' thirty-fifth wedding anniversary party?"

Mom's brow furrowed for a moment. "The big blond? Are they still together? What a pity. You made such a nice couple in high school."

Kenny and I grew up on the same block and ran in the same childhood gang. We also came out and fumbled toward sexual maturity together, eventually coming to the mutual conclusion that we were better friends than lovers.

She tapped her fingers on the tabletop. "I wish you'd find someone, darling. I hate to see you wasting your best years alone."

I raised my eyebrows. "You stayed single for a long time after Papa died."

She waved her hand dismissively. "Bill didn't die. He cheated on you habitually and when you made too much of a fuss about it, he left. I say good riddance. It's a wonder you didn't get something horrid from him."

It was wonderful to have a sympathetic mother, but clearly I'd confided far too much in those first weeks after Bill moved out. "I'm fine, Mom. And I'm okay on my own, just like you were."

She shook her head. "It's not the same thing. I had a child to raise, and women are different. We don't need relationships the way men do."

I laughed. "That would explain the popularity of romance novels."

She shrugged. "That's something I've never been able to explain. And you're dodging the question."

"The question of my love life? Sorry, nothing to tell." I dipped papadum into chili sauce.

"I hope you're not turning into one of those gay men who frequent bathhouses and brothels." She wrinkled her nose. "That sounds unsavory."

"Can we please talk about something else?" I looked frantically for the waiter. Perhaps more food would rescue me.

She reached across the table and patted my arm. "Promise me you'll protect yourself."

I groaned. "Mom, I haven't done anything requiring protection in a long time. There, now are you happy?"

"Why should I be happy that you're unhappy? Maybe you should go on one of those Internet dating sites. Does eHarmony do gay? Or better yet, JDate?"

I rolled my eyes. "How's work?"

She gave me one last concerned look and launched into the finer legal points behind her latest high-profile case. As usual, she was careful not to tell me much beyond what I'd read in the newspapers, but I was grateful we'd moved off the excruciating topic of my sexless life.

Chapter Four

The term final fell on a Monday. Students filed in, their faces set in the same grim terror as the first day of class. Isaac was not among them.

I passed out tests and sat behind my desk, listening to the scratch of pencils and the tick of the wall clock. Minutes dragged by. Students' brows scrunched. Outside the windows, big flakes of snow fell in gentle swirls.

The first few tests were turned in either by the quick or the lost, after which backpacks were retrieved and holiday best wishes expressed. The test period was more than halfway through when Isaac slunk through the door. He kept his head down, but I could see a purple stain across his left cheek.

"Sorry," he mumbled.

I handed him a test. "Take your time. No one's scheduled here next hour."

He nodded and shuffled to the back, walking with the hint of a limp.

Students filed out. Some smiled at me as they handed in their tests. Others lurched by in a daze. Either way, the relief at completion was palpable. Isaac worked on, bent over his paper in concentration. Eventually we were alone. I watched him, noting that he held his arm at an awkward angle and that all his movements were slow, like an old man on a cold day.

When he sat back, our eyes met.

"Done?" I asked, launching myself from the edge of the desk where I perched.

He nodded slowly. "Good test. I missed a few."

"You have the highest grade going into the final. I think you can afford to miss a few." I walked up the aisle toward him. "What happened?"

He touched his cheek, where a purple blotch extended to his swollen eye. "There was a little trouble at the club last night."

I stepped close. I put my finger under his chin and tipped his face up to examine the damage. "You should see a doctor."

He grimaced. "That's where I was this morning. I was afraid I broke my arm, but they x-rayed it. Just a sprain."

I let my fingers linger on his face for a moment, dropped them, and picked up his test. "Must be a rough club where you work."

He shrugged. The gesture made him wince. "The tips are good."

He stood, and I stepped back. "Are you going home for the break?"

Picking up his backpack, he shook his head. "I'm not really welcome there. Besides, I have to work."

He looked so young and vulnerable that I asked, "Do you want to get some lunch and talk about it?"

"Thanks, anyway. It wouldn't be a good idea. People might get the wrong impression." His brown eyes looked old and sad.

I should have disagreed and insisted that he come to lunch. But instead I nodded and let him walk out into the snow alone.

* * * *

Every New Year's Eve, the Marks threw a glittering bash. Melvin Marks had his own dermatology clinic, where he tended to the blemishes of Chicago's best families. The House Built on Acne, Kenny's nickname for the place, was a three-story Colonial with grounds groomed by a host of Hispanic men, some of whom, I'm ashamed to say, Kenny and I spent hours watching during the long summer afternoons of our misspent youth. I'd never understood why Sarah Marks and my mother were such good friends. With her manicured nails and surgically enhanced figure, Sarah was the exact opposite of my career-driven, independent mother. About the only thing they had in common was membership in the local chapter of PFLAG and devotion to their gay sons.

Sarah wrapped me in a perfumed embrace. Her sequined gown rustled and sparkled. "Look who's here," she burbled, pulling me along the corridor to where Kenny stood, resplendent in a brocade vest and tight velour pants.

He rolled his eyes at his mother's transparent matchmaking but embraced me nonetheless.

"It's like something out of *The Graduate* in here," he whispered. "I swear, if one more friend of my folks asks what I'm doing out in LA, I'm gonna tell them I'm in plastics."

I grinned. "Give them a break. They all know your mom wants you home, which is the only reason she keeps throwing me at you. I actually think she likes George, except that he keeps you in California. Is he here?"

"And he's not Jewish." Kenny grimaced. "Or here. He can't get away this time of year. Half his business happens between Christmas and New Year's."

Kenny's boyfriend George ran a big catering company in LA, which left Kenny free to pursue his, as of yet not profitable, writing career.

"Let's get a drink." Kenny linked his arm through mine and led us to the bar. "The bartender's cute enough to make me forget I promised George I'd be a good boy, but unfortunately he's straight as they come. His girlfriend's somewhere around here, serving canapés."

"I like your hair." I gestured to the bleached-blond swirl atop his head.

"No, you don't." He pushed up one gelled side. "But you have to admit, it covers the gray. Something you could consider."

"Touché." I accepted a glass of wine from a tall man, who was indeed handsome.

Kenny sipped his wine and winked at the bartender, who smiled blandly back. Kenny turned to me. "I do wish I could talk you into coming to California. Our friend with the environmental consulting firm is serious about hiring you."

I smiled. "Thank you, but I have a job. How's the writing going?"

Kenny shrugged and steered us toward a corner away from the crowd. "*Comme ci, comme* ça. How's your love life?"

"Still dead." I leaned against a wall, surveying the other guests, most of whom were over sixty.

"Maybe we should revive it." Kenny grinned evilly. "Have you been to the new club downtown? Evidently, if you know the right people, you can get a lap dance with pretty boys who are there to please."

Lap dances? My mother's comments about bathhouses and brothels came to mind. "That sounds seedy."

Kenny smiled. "I know. Isn't it delicious? We could go next weekend."

I raised my eyebrows. "I thought you promised George you'd be good."

He waved his hand, dismissing my comment. "I can look, can't I? Besides, do you think dancers really count?"

I snorted. "I think that's between you and George."

Kenny winked. "A sweet boy dancing between me and George? Now there's something to dream about."

"You are so bad." I laughed.

"Isn't it great?"

* * * *

"I can't believe you talked me into this." I peered at the refurbished brick warehouse. A heavy techno beat pounded out each time the door opened.

Kenny glanced in the mirror and slicked up the sides of his hair. "Oh, come on, you need to loosen up. You cannot still be pining for Bill. It's been years. Honey, I'm all in favor of open relationships, but only if both parties know about it. That boy had the sexual hygiene habits of a muskrat. It's time you got back in the game, and I have just the ticket to help you do that." He held up a business card.

I tried to read it by the light of the streetlamp. "What's that?"

"This is your ticket for a deluxe, Le Garçon lap dance." He flicked it with his finger. "My gift to you."

I stared at him. "You're spending money so some guy can dance in my lap? That's crazy."

He made an exaggeratedly stern face. "Shit, Nathan, it's just a dance. And you might like it. How long has it been since you've been that close to another person? It's not right. I'd blow you myself if it wasn't for George."

"What does a lap dance entail?" I hated how naïve I sounded. But the stripper circuit wasn't exactly on my regular social calendar.

"A great looking guy gets in your personal space and gyrates." Kenny leaned close and whispered, "Come on, what can it hurt?"

I shook my head and tried to look exasperated but Kenny was right, I'd been pretending to be asexual for a long time. A man dancing close? My pulse sped up at the thought. I opened the car door and stepped out.

Kenny joined me on the sidewalk. "Relax. Just a bit of harmless fun." He pulled me toward the club entrance.

The two martinis I'd slurped over dinner had left me light-headed and giddy. Kenny always brought out the teenage boy in me. Too much to drink and the memory of being young and sexually adventurous pushed me through the doors of Le Garçon.

Inside, the music throbbed. Scattered around a long, narrow stage sat tables filled with men in groups, pairs, or sitting alone. Kenny sat me down at a table near the stage and disappeared toward the bar. When he reappeared, he handed me a tumbler.

Slumping into the chair beside me, he leaned close enough that I could hear. "Straight vodka, the best I could do. Bartender says the private dances are in the back. Let's sit here for a while to get you warmed up. You like that one?" He smiled appreciatively at the stage, where a very muscular man clad in a leather jockstrap, cowboy boots, and hat gyrated lazily to the beat. His tattooed skin looked greased, and his jockstrap bulged conspicuously.

I shouted into Kenny's ear. "That's got to be a sock in there."

Kenny mock-scowled back at me. "I'm going to pretend I didn't hear that."

The vodka tasted watered. The bar smelled of sweat and cologne. I could see men in the audience pressing furtive hands to their own crotches, adjusting themselves as they stared at the performers. The man thrusting his hips at us from the stage wasn't even my type, but there was something about the sexualized aura, the pulse of the music, the sound and smell of men watching other men display themselves that began to affect me. Kenny stood and tucked a twenty in the man's jock, his fingers lingering on the fabric.

He winked at me as he sat back down. "Felt real enough to me."

A waiter appeared. Kenny ordered more watery vodka. The song ended and another dancer took the stage. This one couldn't have been more than eighteen. It felt wicked and disturbingly exciting to watch him. He was followed by another, darker man, and Kenny ordered another round.

A gaggle of screeching, giggling women arrived. Kenny frowned and mouthed, *Bachelorette.*

The waiter appeared with our drinks, and Kenny held up the business card and beckoned him down. He whispered in the waiter's ear. The man nodded. Kenny pointed to me. I blushed. Was I really going to go through with this? Kenny pressed a bill into his hand, and the man gestured toward the back. Kenny looked at me, his eyebrows raised. A tremble went through me. He was right. It had been far too long since I'd thought of myself as a sexual being. Before Isaac, I'd thought my sex-drive was simply gone. Atrophied. Maybe if I went through with this, the man who danced for me would be so hot that I'd quit fantasizing about someone I couldn't have. I gave Kenny a nod. We stood and followed the waiter down a hallway. I felt dizzy with vodka, and my cock went thick and needy.

The same music played as in the front room. The pounding beat echoed in my pulse.

Kenny took my arm and leaned close to my ear. "You're not going to chicken out at the last minute, are you?"

I shook my head, and he patted my back. "Good."

We stopped at a doorway. The waiter spoke with someone, turned, and walked past us, back toward the throbbing beat. The door opened, and a large man surveyed us.

"Both of you?" he growled.

Kenny squeezed my arm. "No, honey, I'm here to have a drink. But Natey Boy needs something special."

"You're not cops, are you?" He opened the door wider, and I could see a dimly lit room with soft-looking couches upholstered in red and gold.

"Hardly." Kenny laughed.

I looked at Kenny. Was there something illegal about this? The big man kept looking at me so I muttered, "I'm a teacher."

He grunted and opened the door. "Have a seat. It's a busy night, but I'll see who's free." He disappeared behind a beaded curtain.

Kenny threw himself onto a couch. "How nice, a waiting room. Just like at the doctor's."

I was about to respond when the curtain rustled again. A young blond man in tight shorts appeared, and behind him, a dark figure with a bandaged wrist, wearing low-slung jeans and a white shirt unbuttoned to his sternum.

I shook my head, wondering if I was seeing things. "Isaac?"

Kenny looked from me to Isaac, who seemed frozen halfway into the room. "You know that one? You dog, you. I thought you said you hadn't ever been here."

I looked at Isaac, who stared at me with big, terrified eyes.

"Don't just stand there." Kenny was speaking to me, but it was Isaac who moved.

He took my hand and led me down a short hallway to a tiny booth furnished with a heavily padded chair in the center. A vanilla-scented candle burned on an end table. The music was muted enough that we could talk without shouting, but the pounding beat still filled the room.

"Isaac, what are you doing here?" I asked once the door was closed.

He let go of my hand and stood close. "I work here. You paid for a block dance so you have half an hour. Do you want to talk or get what you paid for?"

I touched his cheek. "Your bruise is gone."

Tears formed in his eyes. "It's your call, Professor. We're not at school now. What do you want?"

I looked at him, our eyes almost at the same height. My alcohol-addled brain slogged from thought to thought. One shocked part of my brain screamed that I should bolt and forget I'd ever been here. But the man I dreamed about every night was there in front of me, mine to take. Touching him would shift where we stood with each other and we'd never get our delicate balance back. On the other hand, simply knowing what Isaac did for a living changed everything, and whatever else we did wouldn't make me forget. As if reading my mind, he whispered, "Whatever happens here stays here."

He gestured toward the chair. I sat, my eyes never leaving his. He stood in front of me, his hips moving in sultry circles as he unbuttoned his shirt and let it fall from his shoulders. My mouth went dry at the sight of his bare chest. The color of his skin, the definition of his muscles—he was magnificent. I watched, mesmerized, as he danced. He slowed, licked his lips, took a deep breath and hooked his fingers in the waistline of his jeans, He ripped them off, leaving him naked except for a dark blue thong.

I stared, open mouthed, unable to tear my gaze away. He caught the rhythm of the music again, moved forward and edged my knees together. His thighs were warm as he straddled mine.

I looked up into his eyes. "Can I kiss you?"

He paused, a smile twitching the corners of his mouth. "I've imagined you kissing me. But never like this."

I reached up to touch his chest. "Me, too. I still want to."

He leaned down to me. Our lips touched, and it was as if a dam broke in me. I groaned and slid my hands into his hair. I pulled him down me, my tongue finding his. He braced himself against the edge of my chair. He tasted like whiskey, and I thought he must do shots to make it through the night. The thought of other men seeing him like this made me angry, and I grabbed his ass and pulled him down onto my lap, rubbing my rock hard cock against him.

He grew still for a moment. Then, as if shifting gears, he met my passion with his own. I reached between us to feel his cock, but he batted my hand away and pushed me backward until I fell onto the bed.

He broke the kiss. "Reciprocal's for dating. You paid for the special, and this is what you get."

He kissed my jaw and collarbone as his fingers undid the buttons on my shirt. He slid off my lap. His mouth was warm on my skin as he licked and kissed his way down my torso. He fumbled with my belt. I closed my eyes and let him serve me. Shame and excitement surged through me in an intoxicating combination. I heard him unzip me, and he lifted my hips and slid down my pants. He wrapped his fingers around my shaft. I felt his mouth on me, and every other thought fled. Opening my eyes, I saw my legs akimbo with Isaac in between. He looked up at me from under dark curls, his lips as beautiful around my cock as I'd envisioned. My heart pounded. Sweat trickled down my back. This was better and much worse than anything I'd imagined as I masturbated to images of this boy, no, this man.

My breathing shifted, and Isaac sensed it. He pulled his mouth away, pumping me with his fist. One finger of his other hand found my ass, circled gently, and pressed in. I came with a shout.

I sat, panting, and watched him move away and grab a towel from beneath the chair to wipe his hands. He didn't look at me as I stood and slowly pulled up my pants.

"Do you do this for all the customers?" It came out before I thought about how the question might sound to Isaac.

"You have complaints? You got what you paid for." He looked at me then, his eyes a mix of sadness and defiance.

"No." I shook my head quickly. "I just thought a lap dance was a, well, a dance."

"Nobody pays that much for just the dance." Isaac glanced at a clock on the wall behind me. "Jack'll knock on the door in a few minutes. You'll need to pay extra to stay."

I wanted to tell him it was Kenny who paid, but what did that matter?

I cleared my throat. "Can you meet me tomorrow, for lunch, to talk about this?"

Isaac shrugged. "What's to talk about? Don't you ever run into students when they're at work?"

I touched his face again. "Sure. But not quite like this. Please?"

His mouth curved up. "Okay, but I can't tomorrow."

A loud knock rattled the door. "Two minutes."

I scrambled in my pocket, retrieved my wallet, and found a business card. More riffling and I found a pen. "Here's my cell number. Call me."

Isaac stuffed the card in his back pocket. He was still sitting on his heels when I left.

Kenny leaped up from the couch when he saw me. "How was it?"

I shook my head. "That was the most astonishing experience of my life."

Kenny grinned. "Well, Happy Hanukkah to you!"

Chapter Five

He waited almost a week before calling. I had brunch with my mother, swam in the college pool, drove Kenny to the airport, shopped for new boots, edited a paper for submission to The Journal of Ecological Research, and tried not to check my phone more than once an hour or think about Isaac's work. I was at home, lying on the couch, reading an article on amphibian conservation, when it chimed. The screen showed an unknown number. It could have been a telemarketer, but my pulse raced anyway.

I sat up. "Hello."

"Um, Dr. Kohn?" His voice had a tinny, uncertain tone through the cell phone speakers.

"Isaac?" I stood and paced to the window, as if I expected him to be standing on the sidewalk outside.

"Yeah. You wanted to talk?"

Yes, I had wanted to talk, but now my mouth felt desert dry, and I couldn't think of what to say. I cleared my throat. "Can I see you? We could meet for coffee, lunch, whatever you like."

Silence. "I thought you didn't date students."

"I don't. I mean, I haven't. It wouldn't be a date. But I need to talk with you." More silence on the line. "About what happened. Please."

He sighed. "Okay. But not near campus where we could run into people. There's a place on Chicago Avenue. It's small and quiet."

I leaned my head against the windowpane, relishing the cold. "Great. When?"

"I have some errands to get done this afternoon. But maybe around four?"

I glanced at my watch. Two hours felt like a long time to wait. "Give me the address."

* * * *

I got to the coffee shop early. It was a long, narrow shop with an old-fashioned wooden bar along one side and tables on the other. A scattering of other people sat with open laptops and cooling coffee mugs. An old Beatles album played in the background. The place smelled of coffee and baked goods. I dropped my jacket across a chair at a table near the back corner and walked to the bar to order black coffee.

Sitting with my back to the wall, I could watch the other patrons and keep an eye out for Isaac. I saw him passing the window, slumped against the wind, before he came through the door. He paused, stomped snow from his feet, blew on his hands to warm them, and looked around the café. I waved, and he came toward me, gracefully negotiating his way between tables, his face an impenetrable mask.

I stood, uncertain how to greet him. Should I shake his hand? Hug? Kiss? He shrugged out of his coat, dropped it on the back of a chair, and with a nod, turned toward the bar to buy coffee. I had an impulse to stop him and insist on paying for his coffee in some sort of gallant move. But it would have looked foolish, particularly in light of my insistence that this was not a date.

Instead, I sat down and watched him talking with the barista. His hands made smooth arcs in the air as he described what he wanted, which must not have been straight black coffee. I couldn't explain the tenderness I felt for him. Somehow, in the time between when I'd last seen him and now, I'd crossed some emotional divide. Maybe it was the shock of seeing a student where no student should be, or the glimpse into the complexity of his life, or maybe the act of sex itself. Whatever had prompted my new openheartedness, I knew Isaac had been wrong. What happened in that room hadn't stayed there.

Isaac set down a mug that had an elaborate heart drawn in coffee and foam. He sat across from me, eyes wary. "You wanted to talk? If you're worried I'll say something, don't be. It's not like I want it broadcast all over campus either."

I played with my coffee cup and stared at a spot between us on the table. "Actually I want to apologize. I didn't mean to invade your privacy."

A sharp laugh burst from him. "My privacy? Dr. Kohn, we had a business transaction, that's all."

I winced. "It's Nathan."

Isaac lifted his mug and sipped. A tiny milk mustache appeared on his upper lip, and he quickly licked it away. When he spoke again, his tone was softer. "I wish you hadn't found out, but maybe it's for the best. Now we know something important about each other. You aren't above buying what I'm not above selling."

I grimaced. "I've never done that before."

"They all say that. But if it's true, we're even. I've never kissed a trick."

I rested my arms on the rickety table between us. He looked pale, and there were dark circles under his eyes. "I want to know why. You're brilliant, one of the best students I've ever had. Why are you...?"

"Sucking dick for dollars?" His mouth twisted into a cynical smile.

I sat back, aware that I didn't like the image of his mouth on other men. "Right."

He smirked. "It beats waiting tables."

"Does it?" I held my coffee cup in both hands and forced him to look me in the eye.

"Like you said, it doesn't pay to work your way through college on minimum wage. Saint Genevieve's isn't cheap." He shrugged. "And I guess now you know that neither am I."

I raised my eyebrows. "Aren't you? I didn't know. My friend Kenny paid. I hope he tipped you well."

Isaac shifted in his chair. "Look, we're good. I got paid, you got what you wanted, and that's that. It's forgotten."

I leaned toward him. "What about student loans? Financial aid? There are other ways to fund a college education."

He snorted. "Right. And how do I pay back Saint Genevieve's tuition on the kind of starting salary I'll get at an environmental engineering firm?"

"You're full pay? What about your parents?"

He shook his head. "Here's a tip you can pass on to other students. Don't come out to your parents until after college. Not only are they not paying, they refuse to fill out financial aid forms, and Saint Gen's has had my emancipation petition under advisement for a year. One full forty-three-thousand-two-hundred-seventy-five-dollar year. Add that to the thirty thousand in loans I racked up my first three years. A good night at the club I take home a thousand, on a bad night closer to two hundred. Either way, it makes a dent in those debts."

I sipped my coffee and contemplated him. "Do your parents know this is how you're making up the tuition difference?"

Isaac looked genuinely frightened for the first time. "No. And they won't ever. They're very religious." He slumped back in his chair. "Besides, we're not in contact anymore."

I reached across the table and touched his arm. "I'm sorry."

"Thanks."

I withdrew my hand and tapped my fingers against my coffee cup while I thought. "Isaac, may I ask you a question?"

He crossed his arms over his chest. "Isn't that what you've been doing?"

I nodded. "But this is personal."

His smile broadened. "The comparison question? Well, it's plenty big, nice-looking, actually, good flavor."

I could feel myself flushing. "No, not that question. I mean, thank you. But what I wanted to ask is why you came on to me—in the boat—I mean. It can't be for the grade, since you're already acing the class."

Isaac's smile faded into a grim line. "What? Because I'm a dancer you think I'm hustling you?"

I raised my hands in protest. "Please, don't get offended. I didn't mean it like that. I just don't get it. I'm too old for you, not hip or glamorous or even particularly engaging. It doesn't make sense."

He sipped from his coffee mug, his eyes softening as he watched me sputter on. When I eventually came to an embarrassed stop, he spoke.

"Now you're fishing. And I think you're being way too hard on yourself. I'm not the first student to have a crush on a teacher." He leaned forward until his face was inches from my own. "I came on to you because I find you very attractive. I sit in class listening to you, watching you lecture, and it turns me on. What can I say? I like smart guys."

Me, too. I felt his breath on my face, and it robbed me of my own. "I don't know what to do, Isaac. I can't stop thinking of you."

He sat back with a shrug. "You know where to find me. I dance Sunday afternoons, Wednesday, Friday and Saturday nights."

I shook my head. "Not like that."

"Private session? I've never done one of those." His smile didn't reach his eyes.

"No. I want you for real." It came out in a whisper.

Isaac looked at me for a long time. He reached forward and stroked my arm. "You were right, Professor. You can't date a student. Or an exotic dancer. Maybe after graduation. When I've quit my job."

He stood, slung his jacket over his shoulder, and walked out without a backward glance.

"Don't call yourself that," I whispered to his empty chair.

Chapter Six

Spring semester started, and Isaac and I barely spoke. Months went by, and sometimes I felt like I'd dreamed the whole thing. That is, until I'd be stopped short in the middle of a lecture by the sudden image of Isaac between my thighs or the tug of the memory of our strange, intimate coffee date. Or I'd be peering through a microscope at a preserved insect sent from California or Maine or Timbuktu and there the image would be of his dark eyes drilling into mine. Then I had to force myself back into the whirl of work.

One day, as I walked into my research lab, I heard his name. Jane and Sue were alone in the lab, busy labeling samples I'd collected over the weekend. They quit talking when I entered the room, and I spent the rest of the day in a sweat, sure that the gossip meant Isaac was dating someone. Later I passed him in the hall, and he smiled at me from under long, dark lashes. I spent that evening in an entirely different kind of sweat.

The final class assignment was for the students to complete a research project from design to data analysis. My office never emptied as students came and went, frantic to design something that could be accomplished in the short time available. I don't allow lab projects. Each design had to take into account the fickle nature of a Chicago spring. Isaac worked alone, his proposed project a study of field mouse genetics that sounded both innovative and complicated. He didn't ask for help. I didn't offer.

Our illustrious department chair Geoffrey Dunn stopped me in the hall before a Friday faculty meeting. "Nathan, you've got to budge on this course thing. It's selfish of you. If you agreed to let the sampling course become an elective, I know others would follow."

I cocked my head and considered him. "And what about the students who graduate without any practical skills? Would they consider me selfish?"

He waved the thought away. "It isn't like I'm proposing the course be eliminated. It could be one of a series of choices within the major."

I nodded. "That's it, isn't it? Your advanced modeling course is undersubscribed, and you think students will flock to it if they don't need to take mine."

He scowled at me. "Of course not. I'm concerned for our students, concerned that we provide them with the best education possible. And if that means more of them learn the basics of ecological modeling, well, I'd be delighted with that."

"Uh-huh." I walked past him into the meeting room. "Because they're more likely to be hired as computer modelers than field-workers? I don't think so. And they agree with me, or they'd already be taking your course."

He sat and began passing out agendas. "We'll finish this later. But consider this, Nathan. Shouldn't that decision be up to them, not us?"

Faculty meetings are brutal enough without starting them in a rage. I could feel my blood pressure rise as I stewed about Gregory's pretense of caring for students. They already were choosing for themselves, I wanted to snap back—they hate your class. Except I knew some of them hated mine, too. Was my insistence that they needed the skills I offered conceit? Barely paying attention to the meeting, a discussion of the administration's new paperwork demands, I prayed I wasn't as pompous and self-important as Gregory. It's a real danger for academics who spend hours watching undergraduates scribble down their every word. Maybe it was time I thought about taking Kenny up on his offer of a job outside the hothouse world of academia. Jenny poked my side and whispered, "Wake up. It's almost over."

I smiled at her. She might be right.

* * * *

Spring semester means planning for the summer break, the only time I can get serious research done. Of the four students working in my lab, only Jane and Sue were capable of working independently. There was a spindly freshman named Ashley and a sophomore named Ted who eventually might mature into the job, but if I hired them for the summer, I'd spend more time babysitting than working. It's one of the frustrating things about running a lab at an undergraduate institution. As soon as you get them properly trained, they graduate and move on. I was delighted when Jane and Sue agreed to work for me for one last summer before they headed off to graduate school.

* * * *

Both Passover and spring break approached. Ever since my first year teaching, my mother has had me bring any stranded Jewish students home for Passover Seder, the ritual meal marking the exodus from Egypt and the beginning of spring. This year I had only one stranded Jewish student.

After class one day, I said, "Isaac, can you stay a minute?"

A smile slid across his face. "Of course, Dr. Kohn."

He gathered his things and stood waiting while the students filed out in straggling bunches.

When we were alone, I turned to him and tried to smile. "Would you like to come to Seder at my mother's house next week?"

His eyebrows shot up. "Whoa, that was unexpected."

I could feel my face flushing. "It's her tradition, actually. She's very concerned about keeping Jewish students from feeling isolated at a Catholic school, particularly around Passover."

He looked skeptical. "I'm not religious. I mean, obviously I was raised it, but the whole thing with my parents, it sort of soured me on the religion thing."

I contemplated him. "I promise you've never had a Seder like my mom's. She marched with Dr. King and takes the whole liberation-from-slavery story very seriously."

He shifted from one foot to the other. "Still...."

I leaned back against my desk. "She's a past president of PFLAG, if that helps."

He smiled. "That explains a lot. All right Dr. Kohn, I'll come."

"Good." I smiled. "You know, there are students around here who call me Nathan, even though they don't know me nearly as well as you do."

He shrugged. "Keeps things in perspective. And thanks for the invitation, Dr. Kohn."

He sauntered out the door and down the hall.

Chapter Seven

The first night of Passover happened to fall on a Sunday night at the beginning of spring break. On Sunday morning, I arrived at my mother's house. She and Jeremiah were finishing breakfast.

Mom waved at me with her toast. "Help us finish this loaf of bread. It's too good to throw out."

"Coffee?" At my nod Jeremiah reached into the cupboard and produced a cup.

When I was growing up, Mom's observance of the proscription against eating leavened bread during the eight days of Passover was spotty, at best. One of my earliest memories was of stopping for cake on the way home from my strictly observant grandparents' Passover Seder. Now for Passover, she cleaned out the cupboards in deference to Jeremiah, who had converted to Judaism sometime in his forties. I hadn't asked whether she still stopped for pastries when she was by herself.

My own faith was complicated. For years, I approached Judaism as an identity more than a religion. But since I had started teaching at a Catholic college, I'd found I wanted to carefully distinguish myself from my colleagues. Not that I was religious. If there was a God, I hadn't met him. Still, I intended to survive on matzo through Passover, and gratefully accepted my mother's delicious toast, since it was the last I'd have for over a week.

"How are you, son?" Jeremiah pounded my back.

"Great. And you?" I took the coffee he offered.

He sat down beside my mother and patted her hand. "Your mother's as stubborn as a mule, but other than that, I'm fine."

She handed me my toast. "Don't try to rope poor Nathan into this. It's between you and me."

I reached for the butter. "You proposed again?"

He nodded. "And she turned me down, again."

Slathering butter on my toast, I grinned at him. "She's a lawyer. There's no way you can make an honest woman out of her."

Jeremiah guffawed. "You probably have something there."

Mom made a face. "Jeremiah Bridges, you were a lawyer before you were a judge. Don't encourage Nathan with his lawyer jokes."

I bit into the toast, savoring the rich, hearty taste. "So, how many tonight?"

Mom counted on her fingers. "Your Uncle Mickey, of course, and Cousin Steve with Cindy and their little girl, Kayla."

At my groan, she admonished, "They're not that bad."

I snorted. "Steve's a prig, Cindy's dumb as a stump, and Kayla is spoiled rotten."

Jeremiah chuckled. "Good thing there'll be four cups of wine."

Mom shook her head. "Grape juice this year. My friend Marla who works at Kaperman Recovery Center is sending over two Jews stuck in treatment over the holiday. I promised an alcohol-free Seder."

I looked at Jeremiah and winked. "Maybe we should do shots before they get here."

Mom glared at me. "Don't even think about it."

I gave in. "All right, all right. No booze. Tell me Cousin Leah is coming. If I have to endure Steve, it's only fair we get his sister, too."

Mom refilled our coffee cups. "Leah's coming, with Pete and the children. Jeremiah met a University of Chicago visiting professor from Israel, and invited him too. An interesting man, a novelist. I think you'll like him. And of course, you and your student. That's fourteen."

Jeremiah sat back in his chair, settling his coffee cup on his prodigious belly. "Tell us about this student. Is he a dim or a bright bulb?"

The image of Isaac was sudden and vivid. I probably blushed. I know I stuttered. "Uh, he's, um, he's very bright."

My mother's eyebrows nearly touched her hairline.

I rubbed my hands together and glanced around the kitchen. "So, how can I help?"

* * * *

When the doorbell rang, my cousins, Steve and Leah, had just started their annual Passover argument about whether their mother's matzo balls sank or floated in the soup. Aunt Deb had been gone so long that even Uncle Mickey couldn't remember how she made the matzo balls. My mother bought hers at Manny's Deli, and most years they float. The two strangers Marla had delivered from Kaperman watched the exchange with the dazed expressions of battle survivors. Given they were in treatment for alcohol or drug abuse, that was probably a fair description of their lives. Uncle Mickey and the Israeli, whose name, Tzvi Nacham, Mom, Jeremiah, and I had spent the afternoon practicing pronouncing, seemed to be engaged in heated agreement about the injustice of Palestinian occupation. The kids were playing an elaborate game that mostly involved running around the house screaming. As the oldest and most obnoxious, Steve's daughter Kayla appeared to be the ringleader. Her younger cousins, Naomi, Lilly, and tiny Seth, trailed behind in various stages of mania.

I opened the door. The only guest unaccounted for stood on the doorstep, awkwardly holding a bouquet. In a black wool coat and pressed chinos, he looked so beautiful that I had to hold on to the doorjamb to keep from touching him.

"Hey." Isaac held out the flowers. "I wasn't sure what to bring."

"Thanks." I moved to give him room to come inside. "May I take your coat?"

"Sure." He stepped into the narrow hallway and shrugged out of his coat. Our hands brushed as I took it from him. There was something electric about it all, Isaac in my mother's hallway, standing close enough that I could smell him. He met my eyes, and I could tell he felt it too, the intimacy of shared space and time.

He smiled. "I'm looking forward to seeing where you come from."

I laughed. "You may not say that after you meet the family. They're not exactly normal."

I led him into the living room and introduced him around. Cousin Steve shook his hand in a very bankerly way, while his wife, Cindy, dithered about how nice it was to have a young adult around. Cousin Leah and her husband Pete were both more restrained and pleasant. The folks from Kaperman muttered and shuffled, and the kids careened into him.

Tzvi shook Isaac's hand formally. "You look familiar. Perhaps I've seen you around the University of Chicago campus?"

I took another look at Tzvi. Had he been to the club and seen Isaac dance? Or worse? I clenched and unclenched my fists, trying to shake off a sudden need to lash out.

Isaac shook his head. "No. Must be someone who looks like me. That happens a lot."

The Israeli gave Isaac the once-over. "I doubt that."

Isaac's smile was forced. He turned to my mother. "Thank you very much for having me."

"My pleasure." She looped an arm through his and led him toward the dining room. "You're sitting by me. I'd like to hear all about how things are going for you here in Chicago."

Leah caught my eye and cocked an eyebrow.

I shrugged. I wasn't about to tell her how complicated things were. We all followed Mom and Isaac and found our preordained places. As I settled into mine, with Tzvi on one side and Leah on the other, it clicked why Mom had insisted on putting him next to me. It was a setup. I could practically hear her thinking, "Both academics, both Jewish, they have so much in common." Only what we had in common was the handsome young man on her right. From the way Tzvi was staring at Isaac, I was sure he'd been to the club. While he might not remember yet, it looked like he might remember soon. I'd need to quickly engage him in conversation The last thing I wanted was to embarrass Isaac in my mother's house. Or myself, for that matter.

Mom clinked a fork against her glass. "I'm delighted to have you all here. Let's get started, or we'll never eat."

My shoulders relaxed as Tzvi's focus shifted to his prayer book.

In my grandparents' house, the Seder meal took hours. The formal telling of the Exodus story, the songs, psalms, prayers—it all went on and on and on. I remember falling asleep before any real food was produced. My mother's Seders preserved bits and pieces—the Israelites still crossed the Red Sea, my second cousins fidgeted and blushed through the four questions, and we all ate horseradish hot enough to make us weep, but the whole thing zipped by at record speed so that we could get on to the important things, like food and conversation.

After the Seder service, Isaac jumped up to help me serve the soup. Steam from the soup pot rose, permeating the kitchen. As we stood together ladling soup, I whispered, "So, Tzvi?"

He paled. "I don't know, maybe. It's not like I would remember most of them. And I don't even register the guys who watch me dance out front."

I winced. "Right."

Picking up another bowl for me to fill, he looked into my eyes. "If we got involved, you wouldn't be able to handle meeting my ex-customers, seeing how they look at me, or knowing what I might have done with them. You know you wouldn't...."

I bit my lip, chicken soup dripping onto the stove top. "It's new territory for me, I'll give you that. But I don't think it would scare me off."

He brushed a finger along my cheek. "I got an internship with an environmental engineering firm in downtown Chicago. It starts right after graduation. Doesn't pay much, but enough to cover my rent."

I was puzzled by the sudden subject change. "That's great."

He arranged the full bowls on a serving tray. "If things go well this spring, I'll have my loans down to a manageable level by graduation."

I nodded, handing him another bowl. I didn't want to think about how he was earning enough to pay off his loans now.

He gave me an exasperated look. "It means I can quit in May."

"Thank God." A wave of relief swept through me that was so strong I almost dropped the bowl of soup I was carrying. Even if nothing happened between us, the thought of Isaac safe felt like a miracle.

Cocking his head, he looked at me. "I still think you won't be able to handle it."

He picked up the tray of bowls and disappeared back into the dining room. I stared at the closed door for a long time, wondering if he was right. I returned to the task of filling bowls with clear, aromatic chicken broth and two, perfect, floating matzo balls.

During the main course—a Moroccan chicken recipe with apricots and almonds, served with beautiful red potatoes and fresh green beans—Mom turned the conversation to slavery and what it meant to be enslaved.

"For example." She gestured with her fork at Steve. "Is the financial world enslaving us, or does money set us free?"

"It's unfair to pick on Steve that way," Cindy whined, batting her big blues at her husband.

Leah snorted. "The financial world enslaves us all. Take, for example, public school teachers. Pete and I haven't had a raise since the economy tanked. And why did it tank? Because big investment companies, like my brother's, let their own greed ruin us all."

"Public schools," Steve scoffed. "Why should you get a raise when all you're doing is babysitting those kids?"

Uncle Mickey's fists slammed against the table hard enough to make the crystal rattle. "Oh, for God's sake, would you two stop it? Grow up, will ya?"

Jeremiah cleared his throat. He had on what Mom calls his judge face. "Historically, slavery has its roots in both economics and greed."

One of the alcoholics spoke, her voice little more than a whisper. "I feel like I've been a slave to my disease." Her friend nodded vigorously.

Isaac spoke softly into the silence that followed. "Maybe the answer to your question is that both are true. If we're desperate for money, it's enslaving because of what we become willing to do to get what we need. Having enough money makes us free to choose our way in the world."

Tzvi shifted beside me. I could almost feel the pieces snap together in his mind. His smile as he faced Isaac was cruel. "True, but financial circumstances needn't make us prostitute ourselves."

Isaac held his gaze. "We're all prostitutes in one way or another. Some are simply more straightforward than others."

I stood and began clearing plates. "So, dessert, anyone?" Leah stood to help as well.

My mother smiled at Isaac. "You're very wise for such a young man. What are your plans after graduation?"

Isaac's mouth twitched, but he didn't look at me. "Actually I've been accepted into graduate school in environmental engineering."

"Oh, that's wonderful." She handed her plate to Leah. "Where are you going?"

He glanced down the table at Tzvi. "I have a few offers but haven't decided yet. It depends on a lot of different things."

She patted his hand. "I'm sure you'll make the right choice."

Jeremiah stood and rubbed his hands together. "I'll have you all know I made a chocolate almond flourless torte that is out of this world. Who's game to try?"

In the kitchen, Leah whispered, "What's the story with your student?"

I shrugged and hurried back out to get more dirty plates.

Tzvi was standing. "I'm sorry, Mrs. Kohn, but I must be going. I have an early day tomorrow. No, no, don't get up. I'm sure Nathan can show me where to find my coat."

As everyone murmured good-bye, I had no choice but to follow him down the hall.

"Seder is a solemn event, don't you agree, Nathan?" Tzvi asked as I handed him his coat.

"Of course. Although we try not to take ourselves too seriously."

He frowned at me. "Is that why you brought your whore to Seder?"

"Get the fuck out." I slammed the door in his smirking face.

Mom appeared beside me. "What was that about?"

"Nothing." I leaned against the wall, trying to bring down the pounding of my heart. "He's a creep."

She made a tsking sound. "I was afraid he wouldn't be your type. I do like your young man, though."

I shook my head. "He's not my young man."

She patted my arm. "An environmental engineer. Very impressive."

I rolled my eyes. "He's twenty years younger than I am, and a student, for God's sake."

"Maybe we could all have dinner sometime soon." Her heels clicked decisively as she made her way back down the hall.

I stayed leaning against the wall, nostalgic for my regular, dull life. Loneliness wasn't really that bad, was it?

But then Isaac appeared and my heart lifted. His smile was sad. "I'm sorry I ruined the party for you."

"What?" I sprang off the wall. "You didn't ruin anything."

He shook his head. "I don't belong here."

I rested my hands on his shoulders. "My mother wants me to bring you to dinner."

He brightened. "Does she? I like her."

"She likes you, too." I ran my hands down his upper arms. "I do, too."

He cocked his head. "Tell your mother I'd be happy to come to dinner. After graduation."

Footsteps approached. I handed him his coat and opened the door.

Halfway down the steps, he stopped and turned around. "Thank you for inviting me to Seder, Dr. Kohn. It was the best one I can remember." And with that, he ran down the steps and began striding away.

Leah's arm curled into mine. We watched together until he disappeared. Then I closed the door.

She leaned her head on my shoulder. "You like him, don't you?"

I nodded. "It's complicated."

"Because he's a student?"

I patted her hand on my arm. "For starters."

She smiled up at me. "You're a good guy, you know that?"

"Thanks for the vote of confidence." I kissed her forehead.

"Thank God you don't teach high school." She giggled.

"I don't know, the kids are too young, but I hear some of those teachers are hot." I wiggled my eyebrows at her.

She pushed me. "Flatterer. He won't always be a student, you know."

"That's what he says." I let go of her arm and turned back toward the kitchen. "He also says I'm not up to it. And he might be right."

Chapter Eight

"I said yes to Madison." Isaac looked up from the statistical analysis he'd brought me. "They offered a fellowship with full tuition and a small stipend. I won't have to work."

We were sitting in my office with the door open. Our knees almost touched.

Madison. A long drive from here. "How about Northwestern or University of Chicago?"

He shook his head. "I didn't apply. No programs in my field, and there are too many people here who know me."

I frowned. In the weeks since Seder we'd come to this odd balance. We hadn't spoken of it, but the promise of May was always between us. It felt like holding my breath. "Madison's over two hours away."

"I know." His eyes were dark pools. It was easy to fall in. "My other choices were Oregon State and UC Davis."

Those were half a country away. I smiled. "Madison's a good school."

"Hi, are you guys doing data analysis?" Thad's voice interrupted from the hallway. "I could really use some help."

"No problem, man." Isaac gathered his papers and stood in one, smooth movement. "I'm done here anyway.

We were talking about grad school. What are you doing after graduation?"

Thad shrugged. "My uncle owns a lumber business in Montana. If nothing else comes along, he said he'd hire me to help with environmental impact statements. I'd rather stick around here, but at least the hunting would be great."

"That sounds cool. See ya later, Dr. Kohn." Isaac sauntered into the hallway, leaving me to readjust my thoughts so I could concentrate on Thad.

* * * *

I looked up from grading papers and there he was, angled against the doorframe, wearing a gray tee jshirt and jeans.

I leaned back in my swivel chair. "You look happy."

He smiled. "I stopped by to tell you I quit my job. Last night was it. I'm finished."

Relief washed through me. "Your loans?"

"Nothing I can't handle. And I bought a car. It's not fancy, a used hatchback that gets good gas mileage." He shifted from one foot to the other. "For the fall. I won't be stuck in Madison on the weekends."

"Mobility is good." The room felt thick with subtext.

"Freedom is better." He looked so beautiful in the doorway, his hands jammed in his pockets and his face radiant for the first time since I'd known him. I wanted to leap up and go to him, but the term wasn't over for another week. I tried to put all that into the smile I gave him.

We beamed at each other.

He shrugged. "Thought you'd want to know. I gotta get to class now."

I nodded. "Thanks for telling me. I'll sleep better."

His eyebrows shot up. "Really? If the thought of me free puts you to sleep, I must not be doing this right." With a wink he was gone.

I swiveled away from the open door and sat, willing away thoughts of his suggestion, which seemed to have awakened my every cell.

* * * *

My hand shook as I passed Isaac his final test.

* * * *

Graduation at Saint Genevieve's was an elaborate affair held in the chapel after Mass on the second Sunday in May. The wind blew my robes against my legs, and my hood flapped behind me as I walked across campus. Other non-Catholic faculty, black robes billowing, scurried toward the chapel. It was the only time we sorted by religion. The Catholics were already there. A robin chirped, followed by the distinctive summer sound of a song sparrow. Small family groups milled around, waiting for the morning's events to unfold with all the drama and pomp that the marriage of academia and Catholicism can produce. I had colleagues who taught at public institutions who hadn't worn full regalia since their own doctoral graduation. At Saint Genevieve's, we donned the robe and hood with such regularity that most of us left the outfit hanging in our offices.

"You look too cheerful for graduation morning." Jenny Karn appeared at my elbow, her short, round body drowning in a billowing sea of black nylon.

I tried to appear more somber. "Nice to have the term over."

She grimaced. "Maybe, but first we have to get through this. I swear, every year it gets harder for me to stay awake from A to Z."

I grinned, pinching the bridge of my nose to intone, "Alison Argonaut, Betty Ashton, Charles Atlas—"

"Spare me." She pulled something from within her voluminous sleeve. "This year I brought a book."

I lowered my voice as we neared the back entrance to the chapel. "Aren't you afraid of getting caught?"

She shrugged, and the book disappeared back into her sleeve. "I'm short enough that no one will notice. Besides, what can they do, fire me for reading during graduation? Please, we have tenure. Lighten up, Kohn. The only thing that could get us dismissed at this point is sleeping with a student." She glanced at a nearby cluster of undergraduates. "Like that's attractive. I'd rather have a root canal than take one of the little darlings home."

"How is Lisa?" I asked. Jenny's girlfriend is a tall wisp of a woman, a social worker who makes the most wonderful, double chocolate brownies.

She smiled. "Good. Home, working on a quilt, of all things. She has the living room covered in scraps of cloth. If I were home, I'd be covered in them too."

At the entrance of the back room we strolled over to join our colleagues in the natural sciences. Faculty clustered with their own departments, preparing for the grand processional.

Geoffrey Dunn glared at me from across the group. "Nice of you to join us. The invitation did say we should be here by quarter to."

I glanced at my watch. "I have 10:46."

"Exactly." He smirked and turned away.

A hush fell over the gathering as the college president stepped to the front of the room. "Thank you all for your attention this fine spring morning. It is a wonderful day for a picnic, and I expect you'll want to join with the families in celebrating our graduates' achievement. We need to thank Mrs. Hilbert for arranging the catering this year." We applauded politely as his secretary smiled and blushed. "Now, although I know we're all anxious to begin the summer break, please remember that our parents are expecting a dignified ceremony. Be attentive to decorum." He scowled at one of the historians—an iconoclast whose red Converse sneakers peeked out from under his robe—and gestured for us to form a line.

The music began, and we proceeded out of the anteroom, around the giant chapel, up toward the altar, past the expectant-looking families and rows of empty seats roped off for the graduates, and into our own seats in the first five pews. Facing the altar, we could hear the students start to file in. Protocol required that we not turn to face them, and it wasn't something I'd ever wanted to do before.

Jenny was right. The graduation ceremony was tedious and long. Especially when you'd been through a great many, or when you were very eager for it to end. The president's remarks seemed particularly dry. I had trouble sitting still through our commencement speaker, a lively woman the students had chosen for her work with the poor. Her words were probably profound, but they simply didn't register.

Eventually it was time to call the graduates forward, one by one. They were separated by department so the faculty could stand in front and shake the hands of each graduate who majored with them. Environmental Studies was a big draw for Saint Genevieve's. Nearly twenty-five young people lined up in their rented black robes and cardboard-topped hats. I took my place at the end of the line of the five faculty with primary appointments in our department. As names were called, students filed past the president and accepted a black, vinyl-cased diploma and the vocal accolades of friends and family. We smiled as we shook the hands of the standoffish and embraced the huggers. Since mine was a required course, I knew every student. Jane Good looked more grown up without her baseball cap, Thad Miller grinned ecstatically, and Sue Taylor launched herself into my arms for a brief hug. All the while, I watched as Isaac Wolf inched forward in line. Behind him, an usher led a handful of French and German majors.

And then Isaac was shaking the president's hand. He approached us with a small smile playing across his lips. He shook hands with Geoffrey, hugged Jenny, shook hands with the next two, and there he was, pressing my hand with both of his.

"Thank you, Dr. Kohn." His gaze met mine. "Thanks, Nate." He let go and trotted down the steps. As we descended to our seats, I pocketed the slip of paper he'd palmed me.

In the processional I pulled it out and read, In case you've lost my number, here it is.

I grinned and patted my pocket where my phone lay. His number had been programmed in ever since the January afternoon when he'd called. I looked for him amid the flock of robed celebrants and their families, searched for him throughout the picnic. But he was nowhere to be found.

It took two hours to disentangle myself from the ritual of photographs and parental chitchat. I shrugged out of my robe as I walked back toward my office, thumbing my phone as I went.

He answered on the third ring. "Hey."

I swallowed hard, and my body woke up. "Hi. Where are you?"

"Home. I couldn't deal with the whole family thing."

I tossed my robe on the chair. "They didn't come?"

He grunted. "No."

"I'm sorry." I leaned against the desk and looked out the window where a finch bounced across the sill.

"It's okay." He sounded tired. "I didn't expect them to be there."

An awkward silence descended between us. I cleared my throat. "May I take you to dinner to celebrate your graduation?"

He exhaled softly. "I'd like that. But I don't feel like being out in public right now. Maybe we could order a pizza?"

The thought of having Isaac to myself, with no barriers between us, sent shock waves through me. When I spoke, my voice sounded husky. "I'll make you dinner. Do you eat meat?"

He chuckled.

I felt myself blushing but refused to take the bait. "Steak?"

"That sounds great. What can I bring?"

"Nothing. Yourself. You're the graduate." As I hung up, my heart was doing double time and my cock was standing at attention. I'd need to do some serious deep breathing if I planned to stroll the aisles of the supermarket without arousing attention. Arousing. Attention. Damn, that didn't help.

Chapter Nine

I stepped back to survey the table. My apartment was small, and the table sat in the kitchen. The smell of baked potatoes and sautéed vegetables permeated the air. Two steaks lay waiting beside the stove, and the salad only needed mixing. I'd done my best, using the tablecloth and napkins my mother had given me when Bill and I moved in together and which had gathered dust in a drawer since he'd moved out. Maybe I'd gone too far with the candles, but I liked how romantic they made the little kitchen look.

The buzzer. I ran a hand through my hair, checked my teeth in the mirror, and opened the door to Isaac.

He held out a bottle of wine. "I wanted to contribute."

"Thanks." I took it from him and paused, struck again by the problem of greeting. Anticipation had left me uncertain.

He smiled. "Can I come in?"

"Oh, sure, of course." I let him pass.

He looked around the living room. "This is nice. It looks very grown up."

I closed the door. "I am grown up."

He walked farther in. "I know. I'm used to student digs, with bad posters and orange-crate bookcases. You have real furniture and actual art on the walls." He turned toward me and smiled. "I like it."

I took in the image of Isaac in my living room. "I like having you here." I gestured with his bottle. "I'll open this so it can breathe."

He laughed. "Breathe? Poor college students don't bring wine with that much life in it."

"You're not a student anymore." I checked the label, an inexpensive Australian Shiraz I'd had before. "This'll be good with dinner. In the meantime, I have champagne in the fridge. We should toast your graduation."

"Whatever you're cooking smells great." He followed me into the kitchen. "This is sweet. You're a romantic. I wouldn't have guessed that." At my look, he added, "It's a nice surprise."

I opened the refrigerator, brought out the champagne, and twisted the cork. Champagne bubbled over the top, soaking my fingers, and dripping onto the floor. I trotted to the sink and tried to contain the mess. I glanced over my shoulder at Isaac. "I'm ridiculously nervous, sorry."

He stepped beside me. "Let me help you with that." Watching my face, he slipped my fingers into his mouth one by one, sucking off the champagne.

I watched him openmouthed. My breath came in gasps, and my cock strained against my jeans. I wanted to devour him, wanted his naked length against me, wanted him right there on the kitchen floor. I took a deep, ragged breath. He released my fingers, and I trailed them up his cheek to cradle his jaw.

"I've thought a lot about tonight," I whispered.

He grinned and reached for my belt. "Me, too."

I grabbed his wrists and brought his hands to my lips and kissed his knuckles. "Will you spend the night?"

He nodded.

I caressed his wrists with my thumbs. "We can take our time."

He looked confused. "Whatever you want."

I poured champagne into two glasses and held one out to him. "I want to toast your graduation, maybe our graduation."

He clinked my glass. "I'll drink to that."

Little bubbles stung my nose. I leaned against the counter and looked at Isaac. "How do you feel?"

He adjusted himself. "You mean apart from the obvious?"

I smiled as I glanced at the bulge in his pants. "Don't worry. I have no intention of sending you home before morning. I'm trying to be responsible, but I'm no saint."

He laughed and sipped his champagne. "In that case, I feel good, glad to be done with the last phase of my life, and excited about the future."

I turned on the stove and began heating my cast-iron frying pan. "When do you start your internship?"

He leaned against the counter. "Not for another week. Until it starts, I'm a free man. How about you? Do you have any academic duties this coming week?"

I shook my head. I picked up a steak, the meat cool in my fingers. The kitchen felt hot with unmet need. I dropped the steak in the frying pan. "You took some time off in the middle of your college career, right? What did you do?"

He poured himself more champagne. "You want the drama-free version?"

The steaks sizzled. The smell of cooking meat filled the kitchen. "There was drama?"

He snorted. "You could say so. I got this amazing opportunity to do my junior year abroad at the National Solar Energy Center in Israel. You know it?"

I flipped the steaks. "Sure, we've sent students there for years, part of Ben-Gurion University."

"I loved it there, real hands-on stuff. A few months into the program, I got involved with David, one of the technicians. I thought I was in love." He spit the word.

I felt an absurd spike of jealousy at the words. One look at his face told me I shouldn't.

"What happened?" I asked as gently as I could.

He grimaced. "Toward the end of the year my parents came to visit. I introduced them to David and told them I was in love and that I was staying in Israel to be with him. Let's just say that didn't go over very well."

"And David?"

Isaac frowned. "Ah, David. He was furious about my big revelation. Turned out he had a wife and kid back in Tel Aviv."

"What did you do?" I filled a plate and handed it to him. He carried it to the table and sat down.

"What could I do? I finished my year in Israel, flew back, and tried to reconcile with my folks, at least enough to get them to pay the tuition. When that didn't work, I came back to Chicago, got a job in a restaurant and another working nights in a warehouse, and tried to save up for school."

I poured the wine he'd brought into two glasses, handed one to him, and sat down across the candlelit table. "How did you get connected with the club?"

"The owner was a regular at the restaurant where I worked. He used to flirt with me, leave big tips, that sort of thing." He shrugged. "Eventually I agreed to go out with him, and the rest, as they say, is history."

I picked at my salad. "Are the two of you still involved?"

He stared at me, his fork halfway to his mouth. "We were never involved. And there wasn't anything between us but business after that first night, which, looking back on it, was more like a job interview than a date."

I swallowed and looked at my plate.

His voice was soft when he continued. "I'm sorry, that was probably too direct. But you know what I did, what I am."

I looked up sharply. "I know what you did, but it doesn't have anything to do with what you are."

He closed his eyes for a moment. When he opened them, the look he gave me was very sad. "That's what I told myself for a long time. But ask that guy at Seder at your mom's house. He'll tell you I'm kidding myself, and you are too."

"He's an asshole." I attacked my salad. "You did what you had to do to get through school. Now it's done. You can get on with your life."

He smiled sadly. "I hope you're right."

"I know I am." I set picked up my wineglass. "Another toast. To new beginnings."

His face brightened. "You don't have a wife and kid hidden somewhere, do you?"

I shook my head. "I have a crazy family, but you've already met them."

He clinked my glass with his. "Good. Here's to new beginnings."

We finished eating, and Isaac considered me. "I bet it would drive you nuts to leave the dishes until tomorrow."

I grimaced. "Guilty as charged."

He picked up my plate and his own. "I'll wash, you dry."

* * * *

Afterward, we carried our wine to the living room. I sat on one side of the couch. Isaac took the other.

I faced him across the single couch cushion between us. "You're so beautiful."

"You're not bad, yourself."

Looking at this beautiful young man who I'd been dreaming about and flirting with for months, I felt suddenly shy. "I'm forty-two," I blurted. I kicked myself. Age was the last thing I wanted to lead with.

Isaac set his wineglass on the table and leaned toward me. "I'll be twenty-five in August. Can I touch you now? It's driving me crazy."

"It's been a long time since I've been with anyone." I ran my fingers through his hair.

"Since December?" He leaned into my touch.

I nodded. "And much longer since anyone let me touch them back."

He leaned forward. "I hear it's like riding a bicycle."

His lips tasted of wine. His tongue entwined with mine, and I sank into the kiss like a drowning man going under for the last time. His torso beneath my fingers was warm and firm. As he leaned against me, I could feel how hard he was. I groaned as he pressed me onto my back. My thigh slipped between his, and we rocked together. I slid my hands under his tee, his skin smooth beneath my fingers. With one hand he cradled my head and with the other, my ass. He thrust against me. My cock pressed into my jeans. I needed to get naked with him, but his breath was quickening, and I could feel how close he was. I grabbed his ass and squeezed as he moved faster and faster. He broke our kiss, his eyes on mine as he thrust once more and held, his mouth slightly open and face flushed. It was the most beautiful sight I'd encountered in a very long time.

He rolled sideways with a short laugh. "Sorry, that sort of got away from me."

I shifted, and he slid down beside me. I stroked his face. "Nothing to be sorry about. That was gorgeous. Shall we adjourn to the other room?"

He laughed. "You forgot to say something about rolling around on the couch like randy teenagers."

I smiled and pulled him to sitting. "I like feeling like a randy teenager. But I'm remembering that I own a bed."

* * * *

The bedroom was lit by a small lamp on my bedside table. I watched Isaac undress, my fingers fumbling with my own buttons, zippers and snaps, fascinated by how his olive skin contrasted perfectly with the tumble of dark hair that ran down from his chest to surround his already half-erect penis and scattered across his long, lean thighs and calves. I watched, mesmerized, while he bent to pick up his boxers. I stared at the flex of muscles in his ass. His lower belly glistened with the leftovers from his orgasm, and he used his boxers to wipe his stomach and threw them on his pile of clothes. He turned to me, his hands spread almost uncertainly, and I wasn't sure whether he was showing me his beauty or asking for approval.

I shed the last of my clothing. "You're breathtaking."

It came out before I could stop myself, and I was grateful when he didn't laugh but instead stepped into my arms, the strong, smooth length of him delicious against me. His muscles rippled beneath my hands, his thigh a long pressure between mine. Of course, he was perfect, luxurious like a yacht or a bottle of fine champagne—an expensive, exquisite treat. And tonight he was mine. Our mouths tangled. He tasted of wine and kisses.

It had been a long time since I felt another man naked against me, and I wanted it to last. Breathing deeply, I prayed for self-control. It seemed impossible in his presence. I walked him backward to the bed and fell on top, my knees on either side of him and my cock rigid beside his. I inhaled the sweat-tinged perfume of him and kissed him long and hard, feeling him stiffening against me. Hard again, quickly. A miracle of youth and desire.

Breaking the kiss, I held myself up so I could look into his eyes.

He bit his lip. "I've been getting regular tests, and I was always careful, but I won't be absolutely sure for another three months."

I kissed him slowly. I pulled back again. "So we'll be safe."

He nodded and looked away.

I brushed my finger across his lower lip, bringing his focus back to mine. "I don't care what we do, as long as it's real. This time you're not selling and I'm not buying. We're just two men giving each other pleasure, okay?"

His smile bloomed slowly. "Okay."

His mouth was beginning to feel familiar as I dived into another kiss. I inhaled deeply, trying to memorize the moment, which smelled sweet with wine and tart with his spent desire. Our tongues twined like old friends while my hands explored the newness of his skin. I brushed a nipple, the knob tight and hard against my thumb, and he moaned into me. I slid along the sumptuousness of his skin, chest hair, his and mine, tickling my fingertips. His cock pressed into my belly as I found the ridge of his hip and rubbed myself against it. Hunger surged through me. I wanted to bury myself in the hot, spicy smell of him.

Isaac reached between us. Lightning coursed through my veins at his touch. I shifted, and his hand closed around me. His long fingers wrapped me in a grip both familiar and exotic. I thrust into his fist, invading his mouth with my tongue. The need to possess rose like a dragon. His fist felt good, but at that moment I would have done anything to slam myself into him up to my balls. I could feel the sweat trickling down my back at the thought of him tight and hot around me.

I took a deep breath and broke the kiss, trailing my mouth in a line along chin to ear, the beginnings of stubble vibrating against my tongue. He shuddered as I found a sensitive spot on his neck. I licked it again to hear his gasp and to mark the spot in my memory. Learning a lover was like learning a language, and I was stumbling through the alphabet of Isaac. I craved him, felt drugged with touch. But I wanted to pace myself, take my lessons slowly, not ram myself into his hand like an adolescent.

I eased myself out of his fist so I could travel down his torso. His nipple hardened to a tight ball as I twirled my tongue around it. I teased it with my teeth and he gasped, his cock jumping against my belly. His breath deepened as he wrapped his legs around my waist. His skin tasted of sweat and, as I moved farther down, of salty, sweet semen.

My mouth watered as I saw the glistening drop at the slit of his penis.

"Wait."

I stilled, tore my gaze from the gloriously engorged head to meet Isaac's gaze. He propped himself on his elbows, a blush teasing up his neck.

He gestured apologetically toward his heap of clothing. "I brought flavored condoms."

"Right." With one last, longing look at his naked cock, I climbed off the bed and rummaged in his jeans' pockets. Pulling out a handful of packets, I squinted at the labels.

He shrugged. "The mint isn't bad, and I kind of like the vanilla. Some guys like banana, but I'm not fond of it. Same with the chocolate."

Nothing could look as delectable as Isaac lying naked on my bed. An old slogan ran through my mind: "If you care about your lover, don't forget the cover."

"You used these for blow jobs at the club? Why didn't you use one on me? "

"Didn't think I had to." Was he blushing? "And I wanted to know how you tasted."

"I know the feeling." For the first time I understood how Bill could have had unsafe sex with strangers. My libido was throwing a tantrum. I didn't want flavored condoms. I wanted to feast on Isaac. I took a deep breath and chose.

"I hope you don't mind, but vanilla seems fitting for me." I tossed the others onto the bedside table and ripped open the blue and white package. The smell of sugar cookies permeated the room.

Isaac grinned. "Believe me, vanilla is great by me."

When I was a graduate student, I taught a non-majors' biology lab—a sort of sex-ed for frat boys—where we clothed bananas in condoms. I'd used them many times before and since, and could, and had, given a lecture on their proper use. Still, I fumbled a little sliding the condom over Isaac. I savored the hot silk of his skin even as I covered it. It occurred to me that Isaac was an expert at this, a professional, while I was the epitome of an enthusiastic amateur. I let my tongue explore the overly sweet length of latex, praying I wouldn't disappoint. His groan helped quell my performance anxiety. Just two men pleasuring each other, I told myself, and breathed in his musk.

The vanilla taste soon gave way to the bite of latex, but he felt firm and thrilling in my hand and mouth. I closed my eyes and took him deeply. It seemed I'd been waiting forever to feel him solid and intoxicating in my mouth. Isaac's hips bucked. His hands drifted through my hair like tropical moths. He breathed my name, his cock hard against the back of my throat, and my pulse raced. I held him tight with one hand, saliva dripping onto my knuckles, slicking the latex. He thrust into me. I could feel the beat of his heart in my fist, and my own heart kept time. His balls slapped against my wrist, and the sound of his breath synchronized with my wet moans and pierced me with spikes of excitement.

I opened my eyes to see Isaac watching me with startling voraciousness, and my own hunger leaped to meet him. I snaked my free hand beneath me, grasping my rock-hard cock. The insatiability in Isaac's eyes might have been enough, even if his balls hadn't tightened and his cock hadn't pulsed and my fingers hadn't found the right grip. The sliding, slippery edge was there, thrumming against my lower lip, quivering through the cocks in my hands, beaming between our eyes, spilling into the condom and onto the sheets, and shattering the space between us.

* * * *

I woke tired and hungry. The bedroom smelled of sweat and sex. Isaac lay curled next to me, his mouth open, his breath morning sour. I rolled onto my side to watch him. A beam of sunlight fell across his shoulder. His hair tumbled in a tangle, and dark stubble graced his cheek. My chest ached with the wonder of having Isaac asleep beside me.

He opened his eyes, lighter than I remembered and flecked with gold. He blinked at me with wide-eyed nearsightedness, and I wondered if the contacts he'd removed late the night before were tinted.

"Good morning." I swept the hair from his face.

Isaac smiled sleepily. "Good morning."

"There's so much to learn about you. I don't even know where you live." His stubble tickled my fingertips as I petted his cheek.

He kissed my palm and rolled out of bed. Padding toward the bathroom, he called over his shoulder, "I share a two-bedroom near school with Jane and Sue."

"Two bedrooms? Do you sleep on the couch?" I leaned in the bathroom doorway.

He chuckled. "Nope. Although Jane does sometimes, when Sue gets in a mood."

"They're lovers?" It never ceased to amaze me how little I really knew my students. "Will they miss you if you don't come home for a while?"

He smiled at me as he spread toothpaste on the brush. "Not if I give them a call."

I nodded, brushed my own teeth, and spit. I watched him brush, rinse, and spit, reveling in ordinary domestic glory. "There's a great breakfast place in the neighborhood. I'll take you there if you like."

"Maybe later." He pulled me back to bed.

* * * *

"Let me take you to breakfast." I stroked the smooth length of Isaac's side as we lay spooned in my bed. "There's a place on the corner that makes good omelets."

"Home fries?" he asked sleepily.

I kissed his shoulder, inhaling the pure Isaac scent of him. "Uh-huh, and pancakes, waffles, French toast with real maple syrup. The coffee's excellent too."

He rolled toward me and rubbed a hand along my jaw. "You need a shave."

I smiled at him. "That would be the pot calling the kettle black. And I dare say we could both use a shower. Let's clean up and go out."

He pulled me into a kiss. His mouth tasted of me. He placed my hand on his erection. "Only if we get to play with soap in the shower."

I closed my fist around him, and he gasped softly. "You play with soap. I'll be content with this."

Much later, shaved, clean, sated, and hungry, we stumbled out into the late morning sun.

I walked beside him, hands buried in my pockets to keep from touching him. "So, next Monday you start your internship?"

"And you go back to the lab." He leaned his head back, his face to the warm, spring sun. "This week will be quite the vacation, won't it? I wonder if you'll still like me in real life."

The sunlight glinted off his hair. He looked lean and sexy in his jeans and tight tee. "Oh, I think I'll still like you."

"Good." He smiled wider.

"Nathan." I turned to see Geoffrey Dunn, my department chair, walking toward us. He looked at Isaac. "And is that Isaac Wolf with you?"

"Dr. Dunn." Isaac extended his hand.

Geoffrey turned back to me. "What on earth are you doing together?"

"Working on a project," Isaac offered.

"None of your damned business," I said.

"And right after graduation." Geoffrey frowned exaggeratedly at Isaac. "As I remember, you're more interested in green energy than aquatic insects."

Isaac shrugged. "I'm interested in a lot of things."

"I bet you are." Geoffrey leered at me. "It's good to know you're taking a special interest in our students. Something the president should know about as well."

"We're not doing anything wrong here, Geoffrey." I spoke quietly, aware that passersby were staring at us.

"And I'm sure that's how the president will see it." A sneer crept over his face. "Good day, Nathan, Isaac. Have a pleasant meeting." He loaded the last word with meaning as he strode away.

Isaac stared after him. "Whoa, what was that about?"

"Faculty politics in action." I stomped toward the diner. "I'm sure that if I call him this afternoon and agree to change my position on our curricular areas of disagreement, he'll forget the whole adventure. Otherwise, who knows what he'll tell the president."

I opened the door and gestured Isaac through. It was late for breakfast and early for lunch, so we had our choice of seats. I threw myself into a booth.

Isaac scooted gracefully across from me. "What will you do?"

I shook my head. "Right now, I'll have breakfast. After that, I plan to spend the afternoon with you."

He flipped open a menu. "I mean about Dr. Dunn."

The place smelled of bacon and burned coffee. I leaned my head against the backrest. "I don't know. I'm tempted to say fuck it, let him say what he will."

"What will happen if you do that?" Isaac's eyes were full of concern.

I shrugged. "I don't know. I suppose if he raised a big enough stink, the president might call me into his office to ask whether it was true I'd violated the morals clause with a student."

"But you didn't."

The waitress brought waters and coffee. When she left, I looked across the table at Isaac. "Yes, I did. And even if we don't count what happened at the club, our being together so soon after graduation looks fishy."

He bit his lower lip. "I don't want to get you fired. Deny it. They'll believe you. Why shouldn't they?"

I picked up my menu even though I no longer felt hungry. "Maybe I should call him and agree to give up my course every other year. There are probably other interesting things I could teach."

"Shit. This sucks." Isaac put down his menu and leaned across the table toward me. "I'll tell them nothing happened. It's not worth losing your job over."

I looked at him, sweet, fresh, and earnest across from me. "Actually I can't think of anything more worth it. Don't worry. Nothing will happen until the fall, and by that time it may all be forgotten."

As I watched him order, it occurred to me for the first time that maybe Geoffrey was right, maybe we should trust our students to make the right choices.

Chapter Ten

"Come on, it'll be fun. And I really need to grab a change of clothes." Isaac held his hand over the receiver and pleaded with his eyes.

I sighed. We only had one more day of leisure before Isaac started his internship and I returned to my real life, and I didn't want to waste even the morning of it. On the other hand, I had to admit I was monopolizing his time and he might be ready for company. And he was right. If I was ever going to let him out of the house, he needed at least one more set of clothes.

I sighed. "Okay. But does it have to be Sue and Jane? They work for me."

He rolled his eyes and spoke rapidly into the phone, setting up lunch. "We'll bring takeout."

By the time he hung up, I was already regretting accepting the invitation. A week of Isaac had me feeling intoxicated. I didn't want the world to intrude yet.

The stairway to his apartment had an old-building smell of rancid cooking and mold that made me oddly nostalgic for my own student days. Isaac bounded up the three flights of steps while I trudged behind, balancing a tray of coffee drinks. With each step I reminded myself that I'd had lunch with students before, even with recent graduates. That one of those recent graduates was my lover was a technicality. Wasn't it?

Jane held open the door. She smiled slyly from under her baseball cap. "Hi, Dr. Kohn."

Oh God. "Please, it's Nathan." I thrust the drink tray at her and stepped over the threshold.

Sue stood behind her. She surveyed Isaac. "What are you wearing?"

He glanced down at the baggy tee and jeans I'd lent him when we both decided his own needed a wash. "Yeah, they're a little big."

Jane laughed. "Ya think?"

Sue was chewing her gum at a remarkable pace. As she leapt from one foot to the other, I realized she might be even more nervous than I was. It was a comforting thought and gave me the courage to extend my hand. "Sue, thanks for the lunch invitation."

Jane laughed again and gestured to the giant bag in Isaac's arms. "I think we have you to thank for lunch."

Isaac grinned and set the bag on the coffee table. "And leftovers for dinner."

An awkward silence descended. Sue cleared her throat. "I'll get dishes."

"I'll help." Isaac followed her into the kitchen.

"How about some music?" Jane gestured toward a set of milk crates in the corner of the living room where an MP3 player was docked between an impressive pair of speakers.

Oh God, the intergenerational music quiz. I shrugged. "Sure, that would be nice."

"I have the debut Gabriel's Sisters album. Do you like them?" She smiled sweetly.

"Um, I'm fine with anything."

Isaac appeared from the kitchen with an armload of dishes. "Don't worry about it, honey, she's being an asshole. There's no reason why you'd know any of Jane's obscure British bands."

Jane's eyebrows shot up at his use of the endearment. I'm sure my blush didn't help.

She tilted her head and considered me. "He's right. They're not very well-known. I had to go to a British website to get the download."

I tried to smile graciously. "You can introduce me to them."

"Great." She punched buttons on the MP3 player, and

the room filled with the voice of a woman singing in a minor key about lost love. Jane babbled on about the group, her excitement growing as she spoke. While the lyrics didn't stun me, the music was haunting, and Jane's enthusiasm contagious.

Sue and Isaac proceeded to unpack the cartons of Chinese takeout. Jane and I wandered over to the coffee table. Isaac flopped onto the couch. I perched beside him, feeling old, awkward, and out of place. Sue handed out plates, and we passed the food around, filling them.

Sue and Jane exchanged a glance. Jane cleared her throat. "You're, um, an item now?"

I nodded uncomfortably.

"I'm sorry," Sue blurted, "but it's sort of weird, isn't it? No offense, Dr. Kohn, but don't you think it's, well, unusual?"

I shifted under her gaze. "Nathan, please, and yes, I think it's an unusual situation."

"Is this going to be all awkward in the lab on Monday?" Jane cocked her head and looked at me. "I mean, do we need to call you Dr. Kohn at work and Nathan here?"

"Call me Nathan all the time. And we can try not to let this interfere with our professional relationship." I spread my hands and tried to smile. "After all, you're graduates now. Which means we're colleagues, and it's perfectly normal for colleagues to socialize."

"Were you…" Sue looked at Jane, who shrugged. "Um, together during class?"

I shook my head vigorously. "No, no, of course not."

At the same time, Isaac said, "How do you think I earned my A?"

We all looked at him.

He spread his arms. "Sorry, kidding. We were good. Nothing happened until after graduation."

I was struck by a sudden image of me kissing Isaac in the dark back room of the club, but decided in this case a small lie might be better than a big truth. I hoped Sue and Jane didn't know exactly how their roommate had been paying his rent.

Jane's eyebrows furrowed. "When did you know you wanted to be together?"

"Enough with the third degree." Isaac reached for a second helping of egg foo yung. "Sue, how's the job search going?"

She launched into a monologue. I settled back a little on the couch and nibbled on my sweet and sour chicken.

* * * *

After lunch, Jane and Sue left to do laundry. As soon as the door closed behind them, Isaac pulled me into a deep kiss that left me panting when we parted.

"That went well." He wrapped his hands around my ass and pulled me on top of him until my whole body covered his. His curls spread against the coarse, blue fabric of the couch. He shifted his legs, and my hips dropped between them, our zippers nestling against each other.

I shook my head. "That was the single most awkward lunch I've ever had."

He raised his eyebrows. "Could have been worse. What if they'd asked if we met at my job?"

"They know?"

His smile faded. "Only that I worked late at a gay club and was damned glad to quit."

I held myself up with one hand so I could see his face, and brushed a lock of hair from his eyes. "I understand why you were there. It's always bothered me when our students graduate with crippling loans. And I don't feel morally judgmental about it. After all, I wasn't above letting Kenny talk me into hiring you, not that I knew it was you beforehand. But I have to confess that I don't like to think of you with other men. I don't like it at all."

Isaac's eyebrows rose. "Maybe I should write a letter to the student paper recommending whoring as a way to raise tuition. And does that mean you want to be exclusive?"

I ran a hand along his jaw and looked into his eyes, amazed again at his beauty. "I don't want anyone else. I'd like it if you didn't either, but given our age difference, it seems a lot to ask."

He leaned close. Our lips almost touched. "That's the stupidest thing you've ever said. You think I haven't done enough sexual experimentation? And think twice before you agree to anything. You may not want me as a steady boyfriend. As you know, I have a past."

His mouth on mine was warm and wet. I sank into the kiss. He tasted of soy sauce. His tongue tangled with mine, sending bolts of excitement straight to my cock. I groaned into his mouth as his fingers dug into my flesh.

"What if they come back?" I whispered, my hand traveling to his zipper.

"That would be awkward, wouldn't it, Professor Kohn?" He grinned evilly. "Don't worry. We'd hear them on the stairs."

I paused, listening for footfalls.

Isaac's hand went to my face. "Don't stop. It's hot to be with you here."

I looked into his dark, beautiful eyes, and at that moment nothing else mattered. I pushed him back against the couch and unzipped his jeans. "Imagine how exciting it will be when I blow you on the couch."

He groaned. "Shit, I love it when you talk like a regular guy."

"Really? I'll work on that." I folded my hand around his hardening penis. "Of course, it's hard to talk with my mouth full."

He dug a condom from his back pocket and handed it to me. "It's okay, I like that even better."

I fingered the condom and stared at the slit of his cock, my mouth watering at the thought of him sweet, salty, and naked in my mouth. "You know, in the unlikely event that you actually are positive, the probability of transmission through oral sex is very low."

Isaac's hand on my jaw was firm as he forced me to look into his face. His eyes on my own were heart-shatteringly warm. "Nate, honey, it isn't zero. You think I could live with myself if I did that to you? You're right. Chances are I'm clean. But we can wait a few months to be sure. We've waited much longer than that with much less than this. At least now we can touch and kiss and be together."

My heart flooded as I watched his eyes. "It's a good thing one of us is mature about these things."

He chuckled. "Not very mature. Didn't you say something about a blowjob?"

I rolled onto an elbow and opened the green and white condom wrapper. It smelled like toothpaste as I uncoiled it over him. I slid down to kneel on the floor between his open thighs, and tasted the tip. "Sort of like an after-dinner mint."

I watched his face as I licked down the artificially sweetened underside of his shaft. Isaac stared at me, his tongue poking from between open lips and his eyes hot and dark. I tugged on the waistband of his jeans. He lifted his hips so I could slide off his pants, his eyes never leaving my face. Even when I closed my eyes and buried my face in the warm musk of his balls, I could feel him watching.

I'd never fantasized about having someone watch me, but Isaac's gaze excited me in unexpected ways. Who was I kidding? Everything about Isaac was unexpectedly exciting. I loved the taste of his skin, the sweaty scent of his balls. I took one into my mouth and then the other. Isaac moaned, grabbed his knees, and spread himself wide for me.

I licked up his shaft and took him all the way in, holding the condom with one hand while I fingered the soft skin of his balls with the other. Isaac's gaze coaxed theatricality from me. I felt like a porn star, bobbing lasciviously on his cock.

I thought of the many times Isaac must have done just this, the many men he'd sucked for pay, and my stomach lurched with jealousy. At the same time I could feel my cock dripping with excitement. I hadn't been entirely honest with Isaac. The thought of him with other men made me hot and hard and angry. I swallowed him deep into my throat, suppressing my gag reflex, reveling in the feel of his cock. I looked into his eyes as I sucked his shaft, and my imagination provided images of pricks of all sizes, shapes, and colors fucking his beautiful mouth. It was awful, and it was so hot I didn't dare touch myself for fear I'd come in my jeans.

Isaac writhed. Bracing his feet against the couch cushion, he thrust into my mouth, his cock making wet sounds as it pounded in and out. A growl erupted low in my throat. Dark emotions surged in me. Hunger warred with rage. I needed to possess this beautiful young man, and I wanted to hurt him. Without warning, I plunged a dry finger into his ass. He cried out, his sphincter spasming in pain or pleasure, or both. I pumped hard and fast, my index finger a poor surrogate for my aching cock. My fist slapped a hard tempo against his ass. I sucked him deeply into my mouth while I buried my finger over and over again. Mint gave way to the chemical taste of latex. Spit dripped down his balls and onto my fingers, providing meager grease for my angry fucking.

Isaac's breath came in short gulps. His balls tightened. I watched his head fall back, his hair slick with sweat. With a shout, he arched up into me. I felt the pulse of his cock through the condom and longed to taste the warm liquid gushing just out of reach of my tongue. He winced as I pulled my finger out of him. I sat back on my heels, and a wave of shame and tenderness washed through me. I was ashamed that I found his past titillating. At the same time, I was overwhelmed with tenderness at the look in his eyes, his sweet, satisfied smile, and the stern protectiveness of that damned mint condom.

I stood, looking away from him in my guilt. "I hope I

didn't hurt you."

He tossed the condom and shrugged. "You startled me, but I got off on how into it you were." His gaze fell on the now-painful bulge in my jeans. "We'll have to do something about that. What would make you happy?" He leaned forward, his breath warm against my shaft.

I stepped away. The last thing I wanted was the picture of his mouth around a cock, even my own. I pulled him to his feet. We stood inches apart, the tip of my cock against his pubis and the twining of our hands our only points of contact. I could hear the beat of my heart pulsing in my ear. Something shifted in me. Anger melted, and the desire to possess transformed into a need to be possessed.

I traced his collarbone with my thumb. "It's my day for wanting what I can't have."

"And what would that be?"

I stroked his chest, dark curls rough against my palm. I held his gaze and whispered, "I'd give anything to have you fuck me."

His eyes closed, and I heard him swallow. When he opened them again, he was smiling. "Do you practice those lines, or does making me crazy come naturally?"

I shrugged, still caught in the thought of him inside me. Isaac kissed me, the pungent Chinese flavor of his mouth luscious after latex. His hands traveled down my back in a long caress that ended at my ass. He kneaded me through my jeans and pulled away. "Let me see what I can do to make you happy. Why don't you go down to my bedroom and get naked? It's the first door on the left. Make yourself at home. I'll be right in." He patted my ass and turned toward the kitchen. When I didn't move, he made shooing motions. "Go, go, I'll only be a minute."

Isaac's room had the transient carelessness of an undergraduate. I found myself blinking at its sheer student-ness. A futon lay on the floor, covered in rumpled sheets, an open sleeping bag the only blanket. Drawers haphazardly stuffed with clothing hung half open in an ancient wooden bureau. Textbooks lay scattered beside the futon. A bedside table had been fashioned from an orange crate. On it teetered the same kind of gooseneck desk lamp my mother had sent with me to college more than twenty years before.

It was a young man's room, and I felt both exhilarated and nervous as I slipped out of my clothing and crawled onto the bed. Pulling back the sleeping bag, I wondered if I should wait for him under or on top of the covers. Of course, with no air-conditioning in the apartment, only the extremely modest would pull a down bag up to their necks. I folded the sleeping bag and dropped it off the end of the futon. The sheets smelled the way Isaac does when he sleeps, warm and a little spicy. Footsteps down the hall. Isaac's voice calling, "Close your eyes."

Closing my eyes, I lay my head on the pillow, my body

spread out on top of the sheets with my excitement more than evident, and listened as Isaac closed the door and padded toward me. He set something on the floor with a clink. His exquisite skin covered mine, his weight delicious, his mouth wet and hungry.

He was hard against my belly. I opened my eyes and smiled at him. "The gift of youth is resilience."

His hand encircled me. "Maybe, but you've got a shitload of stamina. Once we're sure I'm clean, I'm looking forward to having you fuck me until I come at least twice before you shoot in my ass."

I groaned, and my cock jumped in his hand. "You're far too sexy for me to manage that."

"And right now that's not what you're in the mood for, is it?" Isaac's hand slid off the futon. He held a bottle of olive oil, snapped open the top, and dribbled oil onto my balls and into his hand. "This will have to do, since I'm not used to having gentlemen callers at home." His slippery fingers traced my ass. I buried my head in his hair, inhaling the scent of my own shampoo.

I spread my legs, opening to him. A finger slid in, his touch much more gentle than my own had been. It brought tears to my eyes. Another finger. It had been a long time, but Isaac was so sweetly careful that I relaxed immediately and wanted more.

"You could use a condom." I huffed out, lifting my legs to give him more access.

He shook his head, propped on one elbow, watching me. "Condoms break. Especially around olive oil." He pulled his fingers out, added another and pushed deep into me. His thumb slammed against my balls and I arched into him, wanting more. Wanting him.

"Imagine my hand is my dick," he whispered into my shoulder. He brought my hand to his impossibly hard cock. "Feel how much I want you."

He moved so that his body caressed my cock as his fingers buried themselves over and over in my ass. We were a pretzel, his fingers in my ass, me holding on to his cock like a lifeline. His hand plunging in my ass mixed with the heat of his cock and his balls slapping against the fist I curled around him. The rhythmic slide in and out sounded like fucking. He increased the pace, finger fucking me fast and hard, and I abandoned myself to the feeling. He flicked his thumb across my balls with every pass. His free hand was pumping my cock, both hands moving in rhythm with the thrust of his cock in my hand. He looked gorgeous, his long, lean torso shiny with sweat, his eyes hungry on my own. My breath came in gasps, timed to his thrusts, each breath a moan, a plea, a prayer. I felt the orgasm coming from a long way off, a huge wave rolling through me, tightening every muscle fiber, releasing every thought and doubt as I pulsed up toward him.

"You are fucking hot," Isaac whispered.

The thick white promise of our lovemaking spilled into a single pool, coating our hands, and dripping onto my belly.

* * * *

I lay in bed and watched Isaac stuff clean clothes into a bag. My ass tingled, and my heart felt stretched. I felt the tick of moments whipping by. We had the summer, and after that he'd be gone again. I didn't want to waste a minute.

"Bring it all."

"Excuse me?" He looked up, a red tee hanging from his hand.

I gestured to the sparse room. "Pack up everything and bring it to my place. It will give us more time together before you leave for Madison."

He sat on the futon, a round stain of oil on the sheet beside him, and stared at me. "You're asking me to move in? We've only been together a week."

I caressed his knee. "It doesn't have to be formal. You could leave your furniture and keep paying rent. That way you can always come back if things go bad."

"What if you get tired of me?" He ran a hand through my hair.

I leaned into his touch. "More likely to be the other way around."

A slow smile spread across his face. "Okay. We'll try it. It's probationary, though."

"I'll help you pack." I pulled him into a kiss.

Chapter Eleven

"You're coming to my Fourth of July party, of course. And bring Isaac." My mother's voice was crisp on the phone.

I looked at Isaac, curled on the couch, studying a technical book. "I don't know."

"Kenny Marks will be there, with George. I'm sure they'd love to see you and to meet your young man."

I stared at the phone. Damn.

Isaac looked up from his book and smiled. "If that's your mom, thank her for e-mailing me the article on wind power generation in Germany, but don't tell her I'd already read it."

"I'll get back to you about the party, Mom. And we're still on for dinner Friday, right?"

She assured me we were, and we said our good-byes. I hung up and sat down on the couch with my back against the arm.

Isaac snuggled his feet under me. "Your mom's great. You're really lucky, you know?"

I nodded. "We have to talk."

He paled and folded shut his book. "Okay."

I rested my hands on his calves and tucked my feet under his hips. "You remember the guy who came with me to the club that night?"

Isaac shook his head. "Sorry. I was too shocked to see you there to register anyone else. He paid, right?"

I nodded. "His name's Kenny Marks. Growing up, we were best friends."

Isaac watched me intently. "Were you lovers?"

"Briefly, in high school." I squeezed his calves. "Although friends with benefits would be the current term for it."

He stroked my ankles and nodded for me to go on.

"Anyway, my mother is having a big Fourth of July party. Kenny and George will be there. She wants us to come, but…" I stared at his knees, unable to finish my sentence.

Isaac's voice was soft. "You're embarrassed because he'll know about me."

I looked up sharply. "No, or at least I don't think so. Mostly I'm worried that you'll be uncomfortable."

Isaac shrugged. "The club was a popular place. Seems like I'm always running into someone who saw me dance. Or the occasional backroom customer. It won't be the first time someone's recognized me. I'd rather not have that the only thing people know about me, but I'm getting used to it."

My gut twisted at the thought of all those men knowing Isaac in that way. But there wasn't anything to say. I didn't need to inflict my discomfort on Isaac. I scooted forward and wrapped myself around him.

"We should go to your mom's party." His breath tickled my neck.

"Are you sure?"

I felt his nod. "And we should invite Kenny and his boyfriend over to dinner before that. I mean, he's your best friend and all."

I pulled back and looked into his gorgeous face. "That's really sweet of you. Are you sure you're up to it?"

He smiled. "Better to do the whole shock thing here over dinner than in some dramatic moment at a party, don't you think?"

"It's hard to shock Kenny. But he'll be jealous as all get-out." I kissed him.

* * * *

For a long time, Kenny was the most cynical person I knew. Then he met George and softened up. They took the long road into relationship, but for the past year or so they'd been rock solid and very happy. I love seeing them together. Normally I would look forward to lunch with them, but for days after extending the invitation, I fretted. Isaac offered to call and out himself before they arrived, but I vetoed the idea. Maybe Kenny would have forgotten, or perhaps he hadn't gotten a good look at Isaac. The club was dark, after all, and we'd had a lot to drink.

But really, who could forget Isaac? Kenny's eyebrows rose when I led him into the kitchen where Isaac stood at the counter, dressing a green salad.

George, oblivious, held out his hand in greeting. "I'd say we've heard so much about you, but we haven't heard a peep. Very nice to meet you."

Kenny snagged a carrot from the salad. He leaned against the counter and contemplated Isaac. "Actually, I believe we've met."

Isaac let go of George's hand and held out his own to Kenny. "At the club, you bought me as a Hanukkah present for Nate."

I coughed, spilling the wine I was pouring.

Kenny grinned and grasped Isaac's hand. "Yes, I did. And it looks like it was an excellent investment."

"I've quit." Isaac shook Kenny's hand.

I interjected. "Really, we met at school. Isaac was one of my students."

Kenny accepted a wineglass from me, his face all Cheshire Cat. Elegantly folding himself into a chair, he waved his hand. "Do go on. This is fascinating."

George stood, holding his glass, staring at the two of us. "You've lost me."

Kenny patted the chair beside him. "I told you how I took Nathan out last winter, got him drunk, and bought the boy? Well, it appears that this is that boy. Nathan, am I to understand that you're rescuing him from a life of sin?"

George sat, looking a little dazed. Isaac turned back to the salad.

I took a long gulp of wine. "Kenny, you are so melodramatic. Isaac and I knew each other from school before that night at the club. He was working his way through college in the most efficient way available. That's done and school's done. He's going to graduate school at Madison on full scholarship in the fall, and until he leaves, we're spending as much time together as possible. End of story."

Kenny's smile softened. "That was quite a speech. Isaac, I think you've gotten through to that stone-cold, scientific heart. Good for you." He raised his glass and gestured for George to do the same. "I'd like to propose a toast to new love. No matter where you find it, it's too precious to squander."

Isaac smiled, and there were tears in my eyes as I lifted my glass. I should never have doubted Kenny.

"Kiss, kiss, kiss," George called, standing to clink his glass with a spoon. Kenny joined in.

I looked at Isaac and shrugged. He took my glass, and set it beside his own, wrapped his arms around me and dipped me backward into a classic movie kiss. I started to stumble, but he caught me, and we managed to stand again to catcalls and hoorays from our guests.

Kenny winked at Isaac. "Welcome to the family."

George smiled and sat down again at the table. "I'm the slow one in this couple. Start at the beginning. You met at school?"

Isaac brought salad to the table, I got the quiche from the oven, and together we told the story, in fits and starts, from the beginning.

Later, as I showed Kenny and George to the door, Kenny whispered, "He's gorgeous."

I smiled. "You're not shocked?"

"Of course I'm shocked. I'm scandalized that you didn't tell me earlier. What are friends for if not to gossip?" He squeezed my shoulder. "I've never seen you like this."

I looked at him, startled. "Not with Bill? No, you're right, it was different with Bill. You're not going to tell anyone, though, are you? I mean, about Isaac's past."

George put an arm around Kenny. "Nothing to tell. Right, honey?"

"A past is very attractive on a man, don't you think?" Kenny made an X on his chest with his index finger. "Your secrets are safe with me. Although, imagine my mother's face if she knew." At my look, he held up both hands. "Don't worry. I'm kidding. How about your mom, does she know? No? I bet she'd be very understanding."

"Maybe." I shuddered. "It's not a conversation I want to have."

Kenny kissed my cheek. "Don't blame you. You don't want to tarnish her image of the man you love."

I blinked at him.

"Honey, you're insufferable." George gave me a quick hug. "He's a nice kid."

"Don't forget to take your vitamins, old man." Kenny threw over his shoulder. "What with all that sweet young energy to keep up with."

As I closed the door behind them, the L word lay on the floor where Kenny had let it drop. Better to let sleeping words lie, I thought, and walked back into the kitchen to help Isaac clean up.

"What was the verdict?" he asked, hands wrist-deep in dishwater. "Can you keep your rent boy or not?"

I wrapped my arms around his chest and pressed a kiss onto the back of his neck. "It's not up to them. But in case it matters to you, you have their full approval."

His shoulders relaxed, and he leaned into me. "And yours? Do I have your approval?"

I buried my face in his neck and let my hands wander to his belt buckle. "You have so much more than that."

The words 'rent boy' buzzed around my brain like a mosquito. I kept telling myself that I shouldn't let Isaac's past bother me. But it did.

* * * *

That Saturday night, I looked at Isaac, cuddled with his book on the couch. Kenny's jab about vitamins kept bothering me and I found myself wondering if I was forcing Isaac to act like a forty-year-old guy before his time. It was Saturday night and he was young. He should be out having a good time, not sitting at home reading about wind power. Bill's old jokes about me being dry as dust echoed around my brain. The more I thought about it, the more I became convinced that if I didn't spice it up some, he'd get bored and leave. "Hey, gorgeous." Isaac looked up and smiled. "Why the frown?"

"Nothing important." I flopped onto the couch beside him and pulled him into my lap. "Let's go out."

He kissed my neck and trailed his fingers down my arm. "I like it here."

I didn't believe him. "It would be good for us to get out of the apartment".

He ran his hand through my hair and pulled me into a kiss. When it broke, he whispered, "Or we could stay in."

"Hmmm." My well-worn cock stirred, then wilted—dry as dust, dry as dust. "Let's go dancing."

His eye twitched. "Dancing?"

"You know, lots of men in a confined space, moving to music." I pulled him closer and swayed to imaginary music.

He shook his head. "I'm tired. Maybe another night."

Another night I'd forget and we'd end up staying in. Which is what Isaac would remember when he was up in Madison without me—that all we did was hang around the apartment. I'd seem boring compared with all the young men he'd meet up there. I jostled him. "Come on, it will be fun."

"I have to study up on turbines. You know, the report for work." He held up his book.

"Which isn't due for another two weeks." I knew I was acting crazy. But I couldn't stop myself from thinking about how old I was, how young he was and how bored he'd be soon. I pushed him off me and stood, holding out my hand. "It's Saturday night. You should be out having fun."

He looked up at me from the couch. A half smile played on his face. "I am having fun, or I was until you turned into Mr. Party Animal."

Then I realized why he didn't want to go out. I let my hand fall slowly. "If you're embarrassed to be seen with me, we could go somewhere across town."

He blinked at me. "You think that I don't want to be seen with you?" He stood. "Fine. We'll go dancing."

It wasn't the most cheerful acceptance I could have imagined, and when I thought about it, I was sorry I'd pressed the point. I would have been happy staying home with a book. But eventually Isaac was bound to resent being trapped in my middle-aged life.

It might have been fun to get dressed to the nines, but Isaac didn't want to, and I let it go. Besides, he looked great in a tee and jeans. He looked great in everything.

We drove to a bar in Boystown. It was still fairly early, but the parking lot was full. The heavy beat of dance music thrummed as we entered. The bar was dark and the air smelled thick with spilled beer, sweat, and cologne. A cluster of men near the door watched Isaac as we crossed the room, but I couldn't tell whether it was because they knew him from the club or because he was wonderful to watch. Maybe going out hadn't been a good idea after all. I pointed to an empty table near the dance floor and mimed that I'd get the drinks. Isaac nodded and walked to the table, his hands buried deep in his pockets and his gaze on the floor.

When I arrived at the table, a tall, blond man was sitting in my seat, leaning in to speak with Isaac. He saw me, made a gesture of apology, and stood. I passed Isaac his drink and lifted my eyebrows in question. Someone trying to pick him up or…. He shook his head and took a deep gulp of vodka martini, slammed his drink on the table, stood, and pulled me onto the dance floor.

Isaac danced with his eyes closed and one hand or the other touching me. A short dark-haired man danced closer and closer, eventually brushing his hand over Isaac's ass. Isaac shook his head and moved closer to me. I glared at the guy. He winked and danced off.

I pulled Isaac close. "Was he a customer?"

Isaac opened his eyes, looked at the guy, and shrugged.

Another man leered at us from across the dance floor. Did everyone know about Isaac? Or was this the normal dance floor reaction to a beautiful young man? Paranoia gripped me. It seemed like every man in the bar was looking at him like meat. I fought the rage that threatened to engulf me. It wasn't logical to think that all these men had been in the backroom with Isaac or even seen him at the club. I was being ridiculous. Still, I pulled Isaac closer.

But it wasn't impossible that one of them had. The tall blond who had sat at the table with Isaac danced up behind him, sandwiching him to me. He leaned over Isaac's shoulder and shouted to me. "How about a threesome? I'll split the cost with you."

I shook my head and yanked Isaac from the dance floor, holding his hand as I stalked out of the bar. On the sidewalk, a group of guys were smoking.

One of them pointed to Isaac. "Hey, didn't you used to dance at Le Garçon?"

"Fuck off." I yanked Isaac to the car. I let go of him long enough to beep open the doors and climb into the driver's seat. "Jesus, Isaac. Did you blow half of Chicago?"

"It wasn't all sex. I worked the stage there too, you know." He slumped into the passenger's seat. "I told you going out dancing wasn't a good idea."

I started the car and pulled out of the parking lot.

Isaac put his hand on my arm. "Let's go home."

I brushed his hand away. "Maybe you were right and I can't handle this."

He turned in his seat to stare at me. "What are you saying?"

I gestured over my shoulder to the receding club and to him. "All those guys thinking they can have a piece of you."

He snorted. "Welcome to my life."

"And that they think you're my…that I… It's too much, Isaac, too much." I stared at the road, my knuckles white on the steering wheel.

Isaac was silent for a long time. "Drop me at Jane and Sue's."

"That's not what I meant." I looked at him. His face looked hard in the light of the streetlamp.

"Let me out and I'll catch a cab."

I knew it was wrong even while it was happening but I couldn't stop my anger from turning toward the only other person in the car. I wanted to hit someone, hurt someone. "Do you have money for a cab? Oh, that's right. You can go back to the bar and pick up a few bucks."

"Fuck you." I stopped for a light. Isaac jumped out and ran into the darkness.

I drove home, the adrenaline still pumping through my veins. I was wrong and I knew it. When I calmed down I knew I'd feel debilitating guilt. But I rode my rage all the way home.

I didn't sleep and spent the next day in bed, paralyzed by the thought of what I'd said to him, and the knowledge that he was gone and it was my fault.

Chapter Twelve

I dragged myself into the lab on Monday, hoping to hide behind my microscope.

Jane blocked my way. "Sue says it's unprofessional of me to say this, but you're being a prick."

Exactly what I'd been thinking myself. I started to muscle past her. "Sue's right."

"I am, too." She stood her ground, hands on hips, staring at me. "Isaac told us everything, including how you weren't above being his customer."

She might as well have hit me. "He told you that?"

She softened a little. "We got him pretty drunk, and even totally hammered I had to pry it out of him. But that doesn't change the fact that you're a hypocrite."

"I know." I stared down at her earnest young face. "This isn't easy for me."

"You think it is for him? He's the one who has to deal with assholes who recognize him from the club all the time." Her lips curled into a sneer. "And since it's how he paid the exorbitant tuition at this fine bastion of education, you could say that Isaac prostituted himself to pay your salary."

That was a stomach churning thought. "I take your point. Now, can we get to work, or do we need to stand in the hallway all morning discussing my love life?"

She stood aside and with an exaggerated bow ushered me in. "Sure thing, boss."

Sue didn't look up from the samples she was processing, but I could feel waves of hostility emanating from that corner of the room. They mixed seamlessly with my own self-loathing. Isaac deserved better than me. And I didn't want to see his face when he realized that.

* * * *

Kenny picked up the phone on the second ring. "Oh God, I'd love to," he gushed when I proposed we meet for lunch. "George is off with one of his buddies from cooking school, doing some sort of olive oil tasting. That's tasting, not testing, otherwise I'd have gone along. And Mom's doing her ladies-that-lunch thing. I'm bored out of my skull."

"I'll be back around two," I called over my shoulder as I left the lab.

"No rush," Jane muttered, peering into a microscope as she processed a sample.

I found a seat at a corner table and sat to wait for Kenny. The diner had an old-fashioned feel, with wood floors and red-checkered plastic tablecloths. Chicago celebrity photos hung on the wall. I ordered a beer from a waitress who was far too cheerful.

Kenny appeared, flamboyant in surfer shorts and a loud, Hawaiian print shirt. He spotted me and waved.

I stood to greet him.

"God, you look awful." Kenny kissed my cheek. "Isn't that beautiful boy giving you time to sleep?"

I scowled at him.

"Ooh." Kenny sat across from me, eyeing my beer. "And drinking at lunch on a weekday. What happened?"

"I'm an idiot." I tried to focus on my menu. "He's gone."

"Gone?" Kenny signaled the waitress and ordered iced tea. He took my menu and folded it in front of him with his own, handing it back to her. "Bring us two burgers with everything and a giant order of fries."

I frowned at him as she walked away. "Are you trying to give me a heart attack?"

He leaned forward with his chin in his hands. "Darling, letting that boy leave shows that you obviously don't give a rip about your heart. You might as well enjoy your demise."

I rolled my eyes. "You're confusing metaphor with

physicality again."

He shook his head, gaze on me. "I'm not the one who's confused. Now start at the beginning. What happened, and why?"

"We went dancing and ran into men who Isaac, well, serviced. Or at least that's what I thought. Some guys recognized him, maybe just from seeing him dance, I don't know. A guy propositioned us and I assumed he was an old customer but he might just have wanted to get lucky." I ran a hand through my hair. "I keep picturing Isaac with all these men. Every time a strange man looks at him I think they're either propositioning him or leering at me. It makes me feel like a dirty old man."

Kenny sipped his tea. "Poor kid. When he started there, I bet he didn't expect to ever be recognized outside the club."

I stared at my beer. At the bottom of the glass a wet circle pooled on the tablecloth. "He saw it as the only way to earn his tuition."

"That's extreme." Kenny's voice was soft. "How about his parents?"

I shook my head. "Disowned him when he came out."

Kenny sat back, stretched out his legs, and crossed his feet. "Oh good, then your rejection won't be such a shock for him."

I stared at him. "It's not the same thing."

He cocked his head. "Really? Explain the difference. Because it sure sounds to me like you're either moralizing or jealous or worried about what other people will think. Either way, it's a lot like what Isaac's parents must have been feeling when they threw away a perfectly good son."

I looked away. "The truth is, he deserves better."

Kenny was quiet a long time. He rested a hand on mine. "That may be, but he picked you, and the last thing he needs is your rejection."

The food arrived, saving me from replying. Which was good, because I had a terrible feeling that he was right.

* * * *

I didn't go back to the lab but instead drove down to the lake and took a long walk along the Lakefront Trail. A breeze off Lake Michigan kept the relentless sun from being unbearable. Joggers thudded past, music player wires hanging from their ears and sweat glistening on bare skin. Occasional bikers and skaters zipped by. Women walked in chatting pairs, and waves lapped noisily against the rocks. Gull calls and muffled traffic mingled with the distant beat of music. The air smelled of rotting lake weeds, dead fish, and hot asphalt. I watched the fluttering sails of a group of boats heading out from the harbor.

I pictured Isaac as he'd been on the dance floor the

night before, distant, tucked into himself, like he must have been all those nights when he danced, and more, for strangers who didn't see him as a person, but as an object, a pretty fantasy boy with beautiful curls. I slowed. A fantasy boy. Isn't that how I'd been treating him, too? Not like the strong, intelligent, courageous man he was, but like my own personal luxury item. Had I really bullied him into going out dancing because I thought he'd get bored, or because I wanted to show him off, like a kid with a shiny new toy?

The revelation hit me with a wave of self-disgust so strong I had to find a bench and sit down. I wasn't any better than any other man who'd seen and wanted or even taken Isaac. I was just the last in a long line of assholes. And maybe I was worse because I'd shamed him and then dumped him off.

I was the one who should be ashamed, not Isaac. He'd simply been selling a product. I was the one diminishing his humanity. I watched a large woman buying ice cream from a food cart. If the ice cream clogged her arteries, would that be the buyer's or the seller's fault? The kid stationed behind the colorful freezer cart, a tall, black teenager with problem skin, was simply trying to earn some cash, and the woman contemplating her tower of chocolate ice cream scoops, she was looking for a little pleasure on a hot day.

I walked back to my car, thinking of what my world would feel like without Isaac. I'd miss that teasing light he got in his eyes right before he made me laugh, and the way he could find the logical flaw in an argument I hadn't thought out properly. He deserved better than I'd been giving him. I drove to the lab.

Sue and Jane were cleaning up, getting ready to head home. They looked up as I walked in. They silently returned to their task.

I reached for my wallet and pulled out two twenties. I held them in front of me. "Can I treat you two to dinner out?"

Jane looked up, her expression sharp. "You want to buy us off?"

I shook my head.

Sue reached for the money. "He wants to get us out of the apartment. Don't you?"

"Yes." I took a deep breath. "I have an apology to make, and I'd rather not have an audience."

Jane crossed her arms over her chest and surveyed me. She looked at Sue, then at her watch. "He'll be home from work in half an hour. We have a softball game tonight, anyway. We won't be back until after seven. That should be enough time for him to throw you out."

"Thank you."

As they passed me on their way out, Sue whispered, "Good luck."

I was sitting on the front steps of his building when

Isaac climbed off the bus. He slowed at the sight of me.

"Hi." I stood, watching him approach.

"Hey." He fumbled for his key. "What are you doing here?"

I shrugged. "Jane thinks I'm an asshole, and Kenny says I'm a hypocrite."

He put the key in the lock, not looking at me. "And what do you think?"

"That I'm all of that and a fool besides." I touched his back, and he stilled. "Can I come in? I'd like to apologize."

He looked at me for a long moment and, with a nod, opened the door. I shadowed him silently as he trudged up the steps. At the apartment door, he paused. "Jane and Sue have a game tonight. They're probably not home."

"Good." I followed him inside.

"You want a beer or anything?" Isaac started toward the kitchen.

I grabbed his arm and turned him to face me. "All I want is you. I'm sorry, Isaac. I've been stupid and arrogant and jealous. You've always been patient with me and I've haven't treated you with respect. I know you tried to tell me that we shouldn't go to the bar. I ignored you, thought I knew what was best, or maybe I was just being a prick. And when we got there and it felt like every man in the room was leering at you, I felt threatened and reacted badly. Why wouldn't they stare at you--you're gorgeous--but you're so much more than that. You're kind and funny, and the bravest man I know. But while they were looking at you, I kept thinking it meant they'd been with you at the club and I got angry and mean. But, in reality, I'm no better than they are." I dropped his arm. Taking a breath, I started again. "I'm sorry. I've been rehearsing what to say all afternoon, and now it's coming out all jumbled. What I want to say is, please, I know I don't deserve you, but can you give me—give us—another chance?"

He stayed close, looking intently into my eyes. "It'll happen again. Even if we don't go out, some guy will recognize me in a grocery store or on the bus. Or he'll look at me in a way that makes you think that he's seen me or been with me. It's not how I planned things, but it's how it is."

I pushed a lock of hair back from his face. "It doesn't matter. Whatever happened or didn't happen, those men only got your outsides. I want the whole man."

The building shook as a bus rumbled by. "What happened between you and Bill?"

I stilled. "A more interesting guy came along. Several of them, actually. And then I caught something from him—gonorrhea, an oldfashioned dose of the clap, as Kenny put it—and I made a scene. "

His brow furrowed. "Who left?"

"He did. I'm not the leaving type."

His mouth covered mine, sweet and hot from the day.

I groaned. "I've missed you."

He kissed my neck. "Me, too. We should go home. Who knows when Jane and Sue will be back."

I ran my hands down his back, pulling him closer. "We have time."

He pulled back. "How do you know?"

"I paid them forty dollars to stay gone." I smiled at his startled look. "People will do all sorts of things for cash."

"I've heard that." His kiss this time was more demanding. His tongue entwined with mine in a perfect fit.

I led him into his bedroom. A bag of clothes was spilled open on the floor, the sheets were rumpled, the bed was unmade, and I was happier to be there than anywhere else on earth.

Feeling suddenly shy, I unbuttoned my shirt and let it drop to the floor, along with the rest of my clothes. Isaac stood, magnificently naked before me, his skin two-toned from working outside all summer. Dark curls of hair across his chest and down his belly sprang out, stark against his pale torso.

I touched his face. "It's a beautiful body. I'm sorry you

had to sell it."

He inclined his head, his expression hardening. "I did what I had to do."

"You must have made a lot of money to pay down those loans." I ran my finger along his lower lip. "I've been pretending to myself that this was all you sold, but it wasn't, was it?"

He opened his mouth, closed it, and shook his head. I kissed him softly, feeling like I'd stepped into a minefield and needed to take exquisite care.

I ran my hands down his shoulders and pulled him close. I kissed his neck, and he shivered. "I've been worried that you'd treat me like a john when I should have been thinking about how important it was for me to treat you like a lover." As gently as I could, I pulled him down onto the futon.

He lay back. "I'm fine. Nate, it's not like I'm fragile."

"No, you're one of the strongest people I know." I settled beside him and pushed back a curl. "But you've been used like a commodity when you're really a kind," I kissed his cheek, "brilliant," I kissed his neck, "loving," I kissed his collarbone, "amazing human being." He reached for me, but I stopped him. "Let me take care of you this once. I want to touch you places they didn't." Kissing the crook of his elbow, I whispered, "Like here?"

He laughed. "You're right. In the whole year I worked at the club, no one kissed me there."

I licked up the inside of his bicep and buried my face in the fur of his armpit. He smelled of honest, wholesome work. He giggled. I ran a thumb over his nipple, which hardened instantly. He stopped laughing. "No, not much nipple action, either."

I kissed his nipple and twisted its mate between my fingers. Isaac arched into me. I let my hand drift across his chest and down his side, running gentle fingers everywhere except the places a man in a hurry for sex might grope. I closed my eyes and imagined my tongue and hands erasing all the rough hands that had been there before.

I had worked my way down his body and was about to take his big toe into my mouth when Isaac jerked it away. "No toes."

"Ticklish?" I asked, propping myself on an elbow and appreciating the view of Isaac's gorgeous, aroused nakedness.

He shook his head. "Bad associations. Let's just say that there are some people who really should pay for sex."

"Ah." I slid back up between his legs and caressed his perineum. "Can I touch you here?"

His breath quickened. "Oh, yes, please."

I buried my face in his groin, inhaled his rich musk, and ran my tongue from behind his balls down to his anus. He groaned and spread his knees wider. His beautiful ass puckered before me. Kissing it gently, I circled his opening. Isaac bucked into me, his hips gyrating. He really was taking me back. Dark chambers in my heart filled with the scent and feel of him. My engorged cock rubbed against the sheets as I licked and probed him with my tongue. I used one hand to rhythmically massage his perineum and held his hip with the other. I didn't know if he could come like that, without touching his cock, but I was willing to try. I wanted, at least this once, for what happened between us to have no resemblance with how it had been for him before.

It started with a flutter around my tongue. I could feel the pulse beneath my fingers, and Isaac was calling, "Nate, oh God, Nate," and I was following him as the wave crested over me, and the world as I'd known it fell apart and settled into something new.

Chapter Thirteen

In my mother's social circle, New Year's at the Marks' and her Fourth of July barbecue bookended the year. As the Fourth approached, the house filled with red, white, and blue streamers and cases of beer and wine. On the day itself, a small army of caterers arrived to set out food on long tables in the backyard. In high school and college, Kenny and I were enlisted as bartenders, but now she hired that out, as well, and my only job was to open the door to guests and to nod and smile through the small talk.

Kenny and George arrived early. Kenny looped an arm through Isaac's. "This is no place for a young man. Let's get drunk on Nate's mom's fine Californian wine."

"That's not fair, Kenny." I looked around at the assembled guests. "It's not like in the old days when only our parents' friends came. There will be plenty of people from our generation."

He arched an eyebrow at me. "Exactly. Although, come to think of it, some of their children may be here." He winked at Isaac. "You'll probably find them in the shrubbery getting high. Whenever we could get away from the bar, that's what we did when we were your age."

Isaac smiled at me. "You were a stoner?"

I shrugged. "It was the eighties."

Isaac squeezed Kenny's hand on his arm. "Let's go get that drink. I want to hear all about the old days."

I groaned. "Don't listen to a word he says. There's so little to tell that he won't be able to help himself, and he'll embellish everything."

Kenny grinned. "Truth is overrated, don't you agree?"

George gave me a sympathetic glance as they led Isaac toward the bar.

My mother appeared. We watched together as the three of them walked away. "I like your young man very much."

"Me, too."

* * * *

By the time I could wander over to Kenny and George, Isaac was nowhere to be seen.

"Bathroom," Kenny slurred. "Nice kid. Damned young, though. He thinks of ABBA as the group that wrote the music for *Mamma Mia*."

"Perhaps that's not the most important thing in the world." George looped an arm around Kenny. "Even if you are my favorite dancing queen."

I spotted Isaac across the backyard. He was shaking his head violently and backing away from a man I recognized as an associate in my mother's law firm.

I strode across the lawn to Isaac's side and put an arm around him. "Is there something I can help you with, Mr. Peters?"

The man arched an eyebrow at Isaac. "Gone private, have you? My mistake." He winked at me and wandered off.

I looked into Isaac's eyes. "Are you okay?"

"Yeah, I'm fine." He gave me a rueful smile. "He was a regular. It doesn't happen all that often, but it happens."

"Let's get out of here." I looked around to find my mother and say good-bye.

"No, we should stay." Isaac gave my waist a squeeze. "Don't worry. I can deal."

Still, I kept him with me through the rest of the afternoon. The sun beat down on us. The backyard smelled of cut grass and spilled beer, and the gathering got louder and looser until eventually my mother began shooing guests into cabs or onto buses. Among the last to leave were Kenny and George. There were kisses all around with the promise of more time together the next time they were in town.

My mother closed the door on them and leaned against it with a sigh. "That's over for another year."

I smiled. "People had a nice time."

She nodded distractedly. "Honey, will you clean up the yard? Isaac can help me with the dishes."

Alarms went clanging through my head. Kenny might be sure that she'd be fine with Isaac's past, but no one wants his mother to know his boyfriend was a pro. "Mom, we can do the dishes. And Isaac and I will pick up the yard, and you can take a nap."

She shook her head. "Isaac and I have some things to talk over. You start on the yard, and we'll come get you when we're ready."

Isaac gave me a questioning look. I shook my head, hoping I was wrong about what she was up to. They disappeared into the kitchen together, and I wandered into the yard. For the next half hour, I picked up beer cans and paper plates, stacked wineglasses on trays to take inside, and tried to ignore the churning in my gut.

As I tied the last garbage bag closed, Isaac sprinted out to me, red-eyed and pale.

"What did she say to you?" I asked, furious at my mother for making him cry.

He shook his head. "She's great. Really great. And she wants to talk to us both now."

He grabbed my arm and led me into the living room.

My mother sat on one couch and gestured us to the other. I held Isaac's hand and her gaze. He felt fragile beside me, but my anger at her melted before the warmth in her eyes.

She took a deep breath. "Isaac and I have had a nice chat, haven't we, dear?"

Beside me, he nodded and squeezed my hand.

"There are a few things I wanted to say to both of you. First, Isaac assures me you're being safe, is that right? I wouldn't normally pry, and I'm sure that if Isaac was as careful as he claims, there's nothing to worry about, but still—"

I cut her off. "Don't worry, we're safe."

She nodded. "I thought so. And things are much better than they used to be. For years I sent money to an organization in San Francisco that worked for better conditions for sex workers. Then the AIDS epidemic hit, and things got much worse." She smiled sadly at Isaac. "But it sounds like your club had some good policies in place."

He shifted beside me. "It wasn't all that bad, Mrs. Kohn."

She reached across the coffee table and touched his knee. "You must call me Becca, or Nathan calls me Mom. You're welcome to, as well."

I put my arm around him and pulled him close. I blinked back tears of my own as I contemplated my remarkable mother. "How did you find out?"

She wrinkled her nose. "That awful Israeli professor called after Seder. I told him it was none of his business, but today Jim Peters cornered me in the kitchen and warned me that he'd heard a rumor about Isaac. People can be amazingly cruel."

I nodded. "I know."

She gave Isaac a sympathetic look. "It's going to be hard to move back here when he's done with school. Idiots like Jim Peters are dangerous snobs. But, with time, there'll be fewer old customers who will recognize you."

I stared at her. People might forget, but Isaac would always be looking over his shoulder. In Chicago, Isaac would never be free of his past. "Maybe I should start looking for a job somewhere else."

"And leave St. Genevieve's?" She looked startled. After a moment her expression softened. "That might not be a bad idea. If you feel about Isaac the way he apparently feels about you. And you have time—it'll be two years before he's through school."

I suddenly thought of leaving my mother alone. "But what about you?"

She patted my hand. "I'll be fine. I have my work, Jeremiah, and plenty of friends. Sarah Marks is a fool to think having her son near is more important than having him happy. And I do think Kenny is happy with George, isn't he?"

I nodded, my mind buzzing.

"Besides, in a couple of years Jeremiah and I will be ready to retire, and we can move anywhere we like." She smiled. "Feel free to settle someplace warm, but not Florida. I hate it there." She looked at her watch. "The caterers promised to be back by five, and it's almost that now. You two run along home, and I'll finish up here."

Isaac stood. "Are you sure you don't need more help?"

She stepped around the coffee table and embraced him. "I'll be all right. Now get out of here, both of you." She kissed my cheek and shuttled us out the door.

Isaac and I stood on the doorstep and looked at each other. The sun felt thick and hot after the air-conditioned living room.

He smiled shyly. "I'm sorry. I should have talked with you about it first. But she flat-out asked, and what could I say?"

I started down the steps. "She asked about, um, your work?"

He paused. "That too. I meant, she asked if I loved you."

I stopped and turned around. He looked down at me

from the step above. "What did you tell her?"

He bit his lip. He looked young and vulnerable.

I rested my hands on his hips. "I'm head over heels in love with you, Isaac Wolf. I really hope you said yes."

He smiled. "Of course I said yes. You think I'm stupid?"

I grabbed his hand and pulled him to the sidewalk where my car was parked.

"Where we going?" He laughed, trotting after me.

I threw open the passenger door and almost shoved him in. "Home. I need to start polishing my résumé." Sliding into the driver's side, I added, "And I don't plan to get arrested for indecent exposure on my mother's doorstep. If we don't get home soon, that's exactly what's going to happen."

Isaac laughed and leaned in to kiss me. So there I was, like a high schooler, making out in a car in my mother's driveway, and I felt better than I had in a long, long, long time.

Chapter Fourteen

I sat at my scope, trying to see whether the midge larvae on my slide had one or two hairs on its hind leg. As they processed samples at a bench nearby, Sue and Jane nattered on about a movie they'd seen the night before. The familiar smell of ethyl alcohol permeated the room. The clock ticked away the minutes until the weekend. August was rolling by, and soon Jane and Sue would head to Kansas State for graduate school. Isaac's classes at Madison started in two weeks. We'd already found him a room in a house near campus. If his new roommates had opinions about Isaac's graying boyfriend, they kept it to themselves.

I looked up at the sound of footsteps in the hall. Isaac beamed at me from the doorway.

Jane gestured at him with her forceps. "Hey, aren't you supposed to be at work?"

He grinned. "I had an appointment at the clinic."

My heart rate doubled. "And?"

"Clean as a whistle. And three months clean means clean."

Sue leaped out of her chair and hugged him. "That's wonderful, Isaac. We should have a party."

My eyes were locked on Isaac's. Jane shook her head. "I think there's already one planned, and we're not invited. Come on, babe. Let's go get a soda."

Sue giggled. "Uh-oh. I wish I hadn't just gotten that mental picture."

Jane grabbed her hand and hauled her into the hallway. Isaac stepped forward, his test results held out before him.

I stood and stepped into his arms. "I have news, too. That friend of Kenny's called this morning. He's interested in eventually expanding his operation to include bioremediation and would like me to develop his program. I told him I wouldn't be available for a couple years and that we're a package deal, so if he could find something for you when you graduate, I'd take the job. He didn't make promises but thought it might work out."

"Wow, that's amazing." He touched my cheek. "Right now I can't think that far ahead."

He held my face in his hands and kissed me softly. I wrapped my arms around him and pulled him close.

A rap on the door startled us apart. Geoffrey Dunn stood in the doorway, a triumphant look on his face.

I leaned against my lab bench and considered him.

"Good afternoon, Geoffrey. Making lab calls now?"

A sneer curled his lip. "Actually, I was passing by and couldn't help but notice—"

"You were walking in the opposite direction across the quad when I came in." Isaac looked indignant. "Did you follow me down here?"

Geoffrey blushed. "Of course not."

"It doesn't matter." I took Isaac's hand. "You can have your damned, curricular changes. I don't care. And you can take this to the president if you want, but it will most likely embarrass us all. I'll have to make examples of the faculty who have married former students. It'll be in all the papers. Who knows, if it went to court we could make law."

Geoffrey looked from me to Isaac, his eyes blinking rapidly. He cleared his throat. "I see no reason for this to go any further if you're serious about supporting me in the next faculty meeting."

I shrugged. "I'll withdraw my objections. After that, it's up to you."

With a quick nod he disappeared. I turned back to Isaac.

He was smiling. "His mathematical modeling course sucks."

"Good to know." I pulled him into my arms. "Now where were we?"

He cocked his head to one side and shifted his thigh slightly to put pressure on my groin. "I think you were about to take me home and show me how much you love me."

I pulled him closer. "'To the depths and breadth and height my soul can reach.'"

"Oooh, nineteenth-century love poetry from a man of science." He purred in my ear.

I laughed. "That's what you get for falling for a fossil."

"I think there might be some life left in these old bones." He patted a very alive, but boneless, part of my anatomy. "Let's go home now, please?"

"Yes, sir." I covered my microscope and gathered my things. Together, we ran up the steps and out into the August heat.

I'd locked my bicycle in the rack next to the science building. Isaac stood smiling at me while I hefted it out of the slot.

I held the handlebars and looked at him. "I take it you came by bus?"

He nodded. "Straight from the clinic. We'll have to walk."

I shook my head. "That'll take too long." I unhooked the bungee cords from the cargo rack, stuffed them in my bag, and handed it to Isaac. "Hold this and hop up behind me."

He looked skeptically from the rack to me. "That's crazy."

I grinned. "We could try balancing you on the handlebars—I used to do that with Kenny when we were kids."

I swung my leg over the crossbar and patted the rack behind me. "Come on. I visited Amsterdam years ago. People ride their passengers sidesaddle like this all the time there."

Isaac shrugged and settled his butt on the rack. "It's not exactly comfortable."

"Just think, I'll be sucking your cock within ten minutes."

"When you put it that way...." I could feel the shift when his feet left the ground. I pushed down on the pedal, and we moved forward. The bike felt off-kilter and heavy, but Isaac slid his arm around my waist, and I found my balance.

I peddled through the steamy air. A stream of sweat ran down my spine. Isaac's hard chest felt damp and warm against my back, the caress of his arms sent shivers down my belly, and I pumped furiously, anxious to be home and naked. I pulled to a stop by the apartment steps, and he slid off, keys already in hand. He held the door while I carried the bike into the instant cool of the air-conditioned lobby, up the stairs, and into our home. Isaac shut the door behind us, and we were alone.

I let the bike drop to the foyer floor and threw myself at him, tangling my hands in his hair and crushing his mouth with mine. We fell against the door. His body still radiated heat from the ride. The tang of our sweat overwhelmed me. In another mood, it might have sent me to the shower, but at that moment, it made my blood pound.

Isaac's hands were under my shirt, and I grabbed the hem of his tee, stripping it over his head as he helped me struggle out of my own. I kissed his neck and ran my tongue through the valley below his clavicle. Slowly I dropped to my knees, letting my lips trail down his chest, his belly, and into the dark path of hair that led down from his navel. I fumbled open his jeans, pulled down his pants and underwear, and sat back on my heels to savor the sight of him long and hard before me. Isaac's hands rested on my shoulders. I closed my eyes, the moment sacred as prayer to me, then leaned in to taste for the first time the briny cream glistening on the tip of his cock.

His skin felt like velvet. I took him in slowly, savoring every inch. He groaned and ran his fingers gently through my hair. I caressed the supple skin of his balls in the way that always made him open his legs wider and moan. With my other hand, I squeezed his muscular ass cheek. Another day I might have used my fist to spare my throat, but this time I wanted him deep and wet, wanted to feel him slam against the back of my throat. I suppressed my gag reflex and took him deeper, in and out, savoring the perfume of his sweat and the familiar spice of his skin.

His breathing quickened, and his hands tightened in my hair. His hips moved, and he thrust into my mouth. The pressure of my cock straining against my clothing was uncomfortable, so I unzipped my pants and pulled it out. But I didn't want to touch myself. I wanted to touch him. I grabbed his ass with both hands, pulling him into me with each thrust. He tasted oceanic, and I savored the saline bite at the back of my tongue, heard his breath change the way it did before he came. My own cock was throbbing in rhythm with my heart. I could feel it dripping precum onto the foyer floor. I looked up at Isaac. His head was thrown back, his mouth open. A long moan erupted from him, my mouth was filling with savory richness, and I was coming with him, undone by the sheer wonder of Isaac's lush, clean seed pulsing into me for the first time.

Isaac slid down the wall and wrapped his legs and arms around me. We sat together, our breath slowly going back to normal. I began to feel chilled in the cool apartment air.

"Shower," Isaac murmured into my shoulder.

I nodded, and we pulled each other to standing.

"That was…" Isaac started, then trailed off.

I looked around at the scene, taking in my fallen bicycle draped with crumpled shirts, Isaac with his pants pooled around his ankles, me with my dick hanging out. "I know."

In the shower, we rubbed lazy circles of soap across each other's chests and backs, working our way down until we were clean, half-hard, and smelling of lavender shampoo.

I turned off the shower. Isaac threw a towel around my shoulders, hauled me close, and rubbed it across my back. Folding my arms around him, I delighted in the sleek glide as our wet chests touched.

I took the towel from him and wiped steam from a section of the mirror. I turned him around to face it and started drying his hair. "I look like your father."

He laughed. "Hardly. My dad is short, fat, and bald. Thank God I take after Mom."

"Still." I wrapped him in the towel, pressing myself against his back.

Isaac twisted his head to look at me. "This whole age thing is your hang-up, not mine." He grasped my hand and brought it down to his hard cock. "You think I'm faking this?"

I curled my fingers around his cock and turned my head to kiss him. Isaac twisted his body into the kiss. His mouth felt fierce and familiar. He cradled my neck and brought me closer, his tongue diving deep into my mouth.

When we broke, he whispered, "Let's go to bed."

I followed his taut ass out of the bathroom, toweling my hair as I went.

In the bedroom, I turned down the covers and watched Isaac stretch out on the bed, angular and graceful, comfortable in his multi-toned skin—arms and face rich brown from working in the sun, his chest and legs glowing gold from weekends at the beach, and his pale hips and dark pubis a frame for his gorgeous erection.

I slid into his arms and buried my face in his damp curls, inhaling the scent of lavender and Isaac. He pulled me close and kissed my neck, tonguing the tender spot below my ear while he pinched my nipple, sending shock waves straight to my groin. I closed my hand around his stiff, smooth cock. Isaac spread his legs, easing me between them. I could hear him fumbling blindly on the bedside table, pushed myself up, and leaned across him to find the lube. I sat back on my heels, passing the squeeze bottle from hand to hand as I looked at him. Isaac watched me intently while he idly caressed his penis.

My own cock felt almost painfully engorged. Watching him touch himself didn't help. I cleared my throat. "Before we do this, I need to talk about what it means for me. I know monogamy isn't for everyone, and I'm not judging, but…"

His brows knit together. "Didn't we already have this conversation?"

I nodded, feeling a blush crawl up my face. "I know.

But if there's one thing I learned from Bill, it's that I'm not good at sharing, especially if we're going to be together like this."

Isaac sat up, wrapping himself around me. He looked into my face, warmth and amusement crinkling his eyes. "I only want you. I promise. And I sure as hell don't want to share you with anyone else. Now will you please fuck me?"

"I think I can manage that." I kissed him, my cock and heart both full. I pushed him back onto the bed, following like a magnet.

"Roll over," I whispered, lifting up so he could comply. He slid onto his belly, his skin like silk against mine. I placed his hands on the pillow beside his head. "Relax."

I licked my way down his spine and spread his legs wide with my knees. His skin tasted clean, and his muscles rippled beneath my tongue. I paused momentarily to appreciate and kiss the dimples above his ass cheeks. I let my fingers trail down his crack to tickle his opening, and followed with my tongue. Crouched behind him, I ran my hands under his thighs and up his belly. He pressed up onto his knees, grinding his ass into my face, his cock brushing my forearms as he shifted from side to side.

I inhaled his dark musk and pressed my tongue into him, licking this most private place. Isaac groaned and pushed into me. I grasped his cock, which dripped precum onto my hand. Still tonguing him, with my free hand I patted around on the bed until I felt the cool plastic bottle of lube. I sat back and dribbled the glistening, thick liquid onto his ass. Isaac's breath sounded loud against the pillow. Blood pounding in my ears, I circled his asshole, my fingers slipping across the puckered skin. I let go of his cock long enough to squeeze a few drops of lube onto my hand, and when I gripped him again, he groaned. I slid a finger into him and felt his muscle tense, then blossom around my finger. I worked him open slowly, one finger, two, then three, until he was gasping and begging for me to get on with it.

I lathered myself with a thick layer of lube, wanting this first time to be smooth for us both. I dropped his cock and grasped his hips with slick fingers. I positioned myself behind him and pushed in slowly, felt him grip me, almost too tight. He relaxed into me, and I slid deeper and deeper. A hint of sweat began to twine through the scent of soap and shampoo. Isaac's muscles bunched and released as he arched into me. I reached around to clasp his cock again, this time stroking it in long, strong sweeps in rhythm with my thrusts. I could feel his orgasm like a distant wave coming closer and closer. He cried out as it crashed over him. His cock pulsed in my hand, and I held my breath, narrowly avoiding splashing down with him. He sagged beneath me, and I stroked in and out of his ass slowly so he wouldn't clench.

I pulled out and rolled him onto his back. Isaac looked up at me with a lazy smile. I grabbed a tissue from the bedside table, wiped my cock and wondered if it was possible to get blue balls in your forties.

He pushed himself onto his elbows. "You gonna be okay? It may take me a minute to recover."

I lay beside him and made circles with my fingers on his belly. "You think it will take all of a minute?"

He laughed. "Even I have my limits."

Isaac rolled toward me, pulling me tight against him. He kissed me gently and thoroughly. When he pulled back, his expression was serious. "I hate to think of you giving up your career for me."

In that moment I knew in my marrow that I would have given up anything for Isaac. Thank God I didn't need to, at least not yet. "I'm not giving up my career. No matter where we go, I'll still be counting hairs on bug legs. Maybe I won't have students, but there are benefits to that. No more papers to grade, no more faculty meetings, no more field trips. It's an appealing thought."

"I don't want you to resent me." He looked young, earnest, and handsome.

Did he really expect to have a serious conversation with my hard-on denting his hip? "Isaac, honey, the only thing I'm resenting right now is that you're not focused on fucking me, which is what I'd like you to do whenever it is physically possible."

He smiled and caressed my jaw. "That won't take long."

"One of the many things I love about you."

Isaac's grip on my jaw tightened, and he pulled me into a luscious kiss. His tongue slow-danced with mine. I could feel his cock stiffening beneath my hand, and I tugged at the skin of his sac in a way I knew would get the blood flowing. He murmured into my mouth and rolled on top of me, his thigh slipping between mine. His warm, silky skin contrasted with the rasp of stubble against my cheek, and I lost myself in his sounds, his spice, his warmth.

He reached for the lube, and my heart rate doubled. He must have felt how close I was because his fingers opened me up with quick, expert circles. I exhaled, willing my muscles to relax as he pressed against me with the naked tip of his cock. I hooked my knees over his shoulders and spread my cheeks, pushing back, impatient to be full of him. He looked so beautiful above me, bottom lip tucked between his teeth in concentration, watching his cock slide into my ass. Then his gaze caught mine with a look that melted my bones. He held my hips and plunged deep, hitting my prostate with a zing that took my breath away. I was panting and grunting like a wild animal. The room seemed filled with the sound of my breath and the slap of his balls against my ass. Afternoon sunlight streamed across his chest. Isaac fucked and fucked me, his eyes locked with mine. He wrapped his fingers around my cock, and I felt something primal rolling up from my curling toes, like an avalanche, roaring through my veins and exploding through my heart as my cock spurted between us.

The world seemed to take a breath. Isaac's eyes closed, and I could feel him spilling into me, claiming me, making me his own.

He slid out of me and fell into my arms. I ran my fingers through his luxurious hair. Sleep pulled, and I felt myself falling into darkness, suspended in a moment of bliss.

The first rule of ecology is that small shifts beget big change. Everything is connected.

The end

Two years later......

a short

The First Question

Plain, egg, onion, whole wheat, poppy seed or spelt? My stomach twisted in knots as I stared at the matzo display. On some level I knew that no one would really care, but hosting our first real Seder felt like a big-deal, grown-up, serious thing to do and I wanted it to be perfect. For a lot of reasons.

I was the kid who never paid attention while the adults droned through the ritual. One year they caught me passing notes back and forth with my cousin, playing hangman instead of learning about Moses and the red sea and plagues. But these days, Passover meant something different for me. Looked at one way, Seder at Nathan's mother's house had been our first date. Which was the way I liked to remember it. That other first date? Some things are best forgotten.

And now here I was, standing in a grocery store in front of a Passover display that was nestled between tortillas, canned chilies, beans, and rice noodles and soy sauce, with a shopping list and a case of nerves. Nathan was back home cleaning out the spare room for his mom and her boyfriend who would be flying in from Chicago in the morning. l grabbed three different boxes—variety's good, right?—and started shoveling the rest of the supplies into the cart, gefelte fish, macaroons and sweet wine. The horseradish tripped me up again—regular or pink with beet juice? Both. I wasn't taking chances. I'd been planning this night for a long time.

The cart bulged with regular and ritual food. I could picture Nathan's face when I dumped bag after bag of food on the counter. He'd stare at me wide-eyed in that sexy way he had, then shake his head and smile. And I'd go all gooey inside. Maybe we wouldn't make it to the end of putting away the groceries before we were going at it on the kitchen floor. It wouldn't be the first time.

The bill was three times what we usually spent on food. And it was okay. We could afford it. Wasn't that amazing.

I stepped out into the April heat and inhaled the gas-fume-laden air. I loved California, the heat, the ocean, my job, loved the word *engineer* in my title, and mostly I loved the freedom of walking down the street without meeting anyone who'd known me before. I hadn't expected to like respectability. But I did. I loved it—loved our life, our overpriced condo and our grown-up furniture. Our friends had real jobs and even if I was almost always the youngest at any social gathering, it was okay because I was just another guy, half of a couple, a matched set.

I drove into the snarl of traffic. Faces in the cars beside me looked mad or anxious or resigned, and maybe I would have too, if I hadn't spent long winters in Chicago selling my soul for tuition money and another long winter in Madison only seeing Nathan on weekends. Three months before, I'd graduated early, Nathan quit his job and we moved to sunny California and now we car pooled to work for the same environmental consulting company. It was like stepping into the light. I was still blinking from the contrast.

In the empty kitchen, steam roiled from a pot of water boiling on the stove. A carton of eggs sat next to it. The balcony door was open and there stood Nathan, beating the guest room rug, his hair a dark halo in the sunlight and a deep furrow between his eyebrows as he squinted against the dust. I watched him. Even after two years, having Nathan in my life felt like a miracle. My Nate. The professor—smart, sexy and all mine.

He glanced up and smiled. I loved the way he looked at me with those dark, kind eyes. Like I was special. Like I was worthy. Like he thought I was a prize, too.

The water. Hard boiled eggs for tomorrow. I dropped in a dozen eggs, turned off the burner and walked into the living room. Nathan came in from the balcony, meeting me halfway for a hug and kiss too long and deep for the hour I'd been away.

"I bought too much matzo," I told him when we pulled

apart.

"Egg?"

"Among other things."

"Mom loves you. There's nothing to worry about." He brushed hair out of my face. It was getting too long, the curls too wild, but there didn't ever seem time to get it cut. Besides, he liked it. He kissed me again, this time sweet and slow.

When the kiss broke, I looked into his deep brown eyes. It was right there on the tip of my tongue. Had been for months. "Nate…"

The timer beeped.

"Is that the eggs?" He pulled away and strode toward the kitchen. "We should peel them now. Getting the shells off is tricky once the albumen has cooled."

God I loved him.

I trailed him to the kitchen. He dumped the hot water and ran cold into the pan. I leaned against the counter, chewing on my unspoken words.

He handed me an egg to peel. It was warm. "Nate?"

"Hmm?" He frowned down at the egg in his hand as

some of the white chipped off with the shell.

It was like diving into the ocean from a high rock. You had to just jump.

"What is it?" Nathan stopped peeling and looked at me, his fingers still in the icy water.

I took a deep breath and leapt. "I think we should get married."

He dropped his egg and stared at me.

I rushed on before he could say no. "It's legal here and we already have a joint checking account and, um, it would be good for our taxes." I could hear the whine creeping into my voice and shut up.

Nathan didn't say anything. He pulled his hands out of the water, reached for a dish towel and dried them. He folded and set the towel on the counter and looked at me, that furrow between his eyes back again.

"You think we should get married for the taxes?"

"No." I leaned forward, not touching him but wanting to. "No. I want to marry you because you're it for me. The one man I can see myself loving forever. You're my heart. My home. I just thought you'd find the taxes argument more convincing."

His eyes went wide. He shook his head and smiled. "I'm a lot older than you. When I'm sixty-five you'll be—"

"—Twenty years older than I am now and it still won't matter. We get to change our names when we get married, but not our ages." I put my right hand over his heart and took his hand with my left. "I thought about making a big proposal at dinner tomorrow night, down on one knee and everything, but I decided you wouldn't like that. So now, over a pot of unpeeled hard-boiled eggs, I'm asking you, Nathan Kohn, if you'll make an honest man out of me."

"You've always been that." He caressed my jaw, his eyes searching mine. "Are you serious?"

I nodded.

His face split into a wide smile that went all the way up into his eyes. He wrapped his arms around me and drew me into a long, deep, whole-body kiss.

I guessed that was a yes.

Fields of Gold

by Dev Bentham

Chapter One

Market booths lined the eight blocks around the Capitol Square. They faced the dense throng of shoppers pushing strollers, walking dogs, and trudging the sidewalk looking for plants, produce, baked goods, free-range meats, artisan-crafted cheeses, jewelry, and soap. Traffic inched along outside, pausing for pedestrians who seemed to emerge at random from between booths to stroll across the street in search of cash, coffee, or their cars. Even the bike lane felt crowded. I slowed to let a swarm of spandex-clad enthusiasts fly by and stopped to wait for a bus to pull out.

It took a few minutes before I could slide back into the stream, but as I headed down the hill, I picked up speed. I rounded the corner where abortion activists warred with green-shirted environmentalists for space. Half a block down, my attention was caught by a sudden flash of very white teeth and blond curls. When I looked back at the road, a man carrying two bushy tomato plants stepped out from between two cars. I swerved to miss him. A car horn blared, and I got a glimpse of a giant black SUV bearing down on me from the outside lane just before it grazed my back tire, throwing me out of control. My bike bounced over the curb and into a tree.

I went nose over handlebars and tumbled through the crowd to land at the gorgeous, smiling man's feet. The fall hurt, and not just my pride.

"Oh my God, are you okay?" His eyes were wide and the loveliest shade of blue. He'd dropped to his knees beside me, and I would have liked to make a joke about going down and knees, except all I could do was hold my ankle and try not to moan. Other faces peered down at me. A woman shouldered her way through the crowd, muttering something about being a doctor.

"I'm fine." I dropped my leg and tried to sit up. Pain spiked through me, and I almost lost my breakfast, which would have completed my humiliation.

The woman pushed me back down. "I'm Dr. Goldstein. Relax. Let me take a look. Pete, see what you can do to make him comfortable."

Pete must have been the man beside me with the wonderful smile because he slid what looked like a wadded-up jacket under my head. I gritted my teeth and tried not to cry out as she pulled off my shoe, poked, and prodded. Staring up at the gathering of Saturday morning shoppers, I prayed for someone to say, "Move along. Nothing to see here."

Pete raised his voice. "Logan, haul his bike over to the stall. It's blocking traffic." He beamed those beautiful teeth at the crowd. "Thanks, everyone. I think we've got it here."

People nodded, murmured, gaped a little more, and shuffled off.

"Thanks," I managed to get out before Dr. Goldstein gave my ankle a particularly painful twist and I almost blacked out.

Pete looked down at me. Dazzling, that smile, almost enough to let me forget the pain.

I held his gaze. He held mine.

His smile widened. "No problem. Haven't had a guy fall at my feet like that in quite some time."

Dr. Goldstein snorted and took my arm. "Let's get you up and see if that ankle can hold any weight."

Pete grabbed my other arm, and between them they managed to get me to my feet. My ankle hurt, but it held, and Pete's hand on my arm was pleasantly distracting. They steered me over to a chair by Pete's booth. Dr. Goldstein squatted and propped my naked foot on an upside-down five-gallon bucket. She turned to Pete. "Do you have any ice?"

"Sure." He started scooping ice from a cooler into a plastic produce bag.

When it was about half-full, Dr. Goldstein draped it over my ankle and gave me a firm, motherly look. "It appears to be a bad sprain. My guess is at least second, if not third degree. What's your insurance situation?"

I frowned. "Two-hundred-dollar deductible, ten percent after that. I don't really have two hundred dollars. I'd rather not get the medical profession involved, no offense."

She stood, brushing off her slacks. "None taken. I'd prefer we adopt the Canadian system myself. I doubt anything's broken, but of course, I can't be certain without an X-ray. You'll want to wrap your foot, ice that ankle for fifteen minutes several times a day, keep off it, and elevate it for the next few days. Try not to let it stiffen up. Writing the alphabet with your toes is one common exercise for sprained ankles. If the swelling doesn't go down and it's still too painful to get around on, you'll have to come in." She handed me her business card. "Call my office. That will be cheaper than an emergency room visit."

I stared at the business card in my hand. Dr. Stella Goldstein. "Thanks. That's really nice of you."

Dr. Goldstein glanced at Pete. "No problem. Jakobsen's has the best produce in the market. Any friend of theirs is a friend of mine."

With a grin, Pete held out a large carton of raspberries. "On the house. Thanks, Doc."

She took the berries and held them close to her nose. "These smell absolutely wonderful. And they're gorgeous— so red. Thank you." She nodded toward me. "Get that ankle taped, and don't let him move around too much."

Pete actually winked at me as he assured her that I wasn't going anywhere soon. *Ooh, sassy.* After she wandered away, Pete called over the scrawny, dark-haired middle schooler who was leaning my twisted bike against the back of the produce booth.

Pete pulled a wallet out of his jeans pocket. "Logan, I need you to run over to the drugstore and get an elastic bandage."

The only reason I'd braved the Saturday market traffic in the first place was to get to the bank in time to transfer the last of my savings to cover the check I'd already sent, the one that would pay my cell phone bill through the summer. At least I'd managed to get the deposit in before the accident. It would be another three months before I got a paycheck. I had a roof over my head, a phone, and not much else. But appearances to the contrary, I had my pride. I struggled onto one hip, reaching for my own back pocket. "You don't have to pay for that."

Pete settled a hand on my shoulder and pushed me back down. "You can pay me back later. You got a name?"

His hand felt warm and strong. I turned toward him and noticed the golden hair covering his deeply tanned forearm. I tried to smile up at him, but my ankle really hurt and my expression probably looked more like a grimace. I cleared my throat. "Avi Rosen."

He nodded, his hand still gentle on my shoulder. He

smelled like sunshine and green plants. "Pete Jakobsen. And that little whip-poor-will is my nephew, Logan, who's about to get us all a lemonade on his way back from the drugstore." He handed his nephew a bill. Logan sprinted in the direction of State Street.

A large woman pushing a baby stroller pulled up to the produce booth, and I looked at Pete's wares for the first time. Rows of cardboard containers stamped JAKOBSEN in bold letters, filled with peas, potatoes, zucchini, blueberries, blackberries, and raspberries covered one side of the table. Turnips mounded between a stack of rhubarb stalks and several huge bins overflowing with various kinds of lettuces. Buckets of flower bouquets sat on the ground in front of the booth.

I watched Pete interacting with his customer, feeling my heart rate slow and that shaky, shocky feeling dissipate. Broad-shouldered and muscular, he towered over the mother as she pointed to containers, which he settled gently on the scale, all the time keeping up a laughing banter that had her batting her eyelashes at him. I couldn't help thinking of the feel of his hand on my shoulder. *Dream on, honey. This one plays for my team.*

Despite the pain in my ankle, it was pleasant sitting beside the booth, watching Pete weigh produce and make change. Somehow the fair exchange of goods seemed pure. I felt that way about teaching—that it was a clean trading of ideas. Research, on the other hand, was more about untangling moldy string—the bits often fell apart in my fingers.

What did it mean that I was a little relieved to be grounded in this sunny place for the morning, unable to get to the library and whack away again at the notes for my long overdue dissertation?

The crowd inched by in a perpetual circle around the capitol, and by the time Logan reappeared with beverages and bandage, Pete had sold a few dozen bags of food. Logan pressed a red-and-white paper cup, sweaty with condensation, into my hand. I took a long refreshing gulp.

"Thanks, kid." Pete accepted his cup and patted Logan's back. "Take over the booth, will ya, while I wrap our patient's foot."

"You don't have to do that." I leaned forward, reaching for the packaged bandage.

Pete held it out of my reach, like a big kid playing keep-away. I stopped flailing around and tried to regain my dignity. "You have a thing for rescuing people or something?"

He set his drink on the ground, squatted in front of my bucket-propped foot, and slid off the melted ice pack. "Beats having you sue me. You wouldn't believe what my liability insurance rates are, and that's without any claims."

I stared at him. "Sue you?"

The firm hand he ran along my calf, pushing up my jeans, sent a shiver up my leg. "This is the capitol. Everyone's a lawyer. You can't be too careful." He looked up at me from under pale gold lashes. I've always been a sucker for freckles. The bandage wrapping crackled. I blinked and refocused on what he was saying, which turned out to be just as enticing. "Besides, I was staring at you and picturing how good you'd look in racer spandex. Who knows, maybe you were looking at me instead of paying attention to the road." He fluttered his eyelids at me. "I can always hope."

I winced as he pulled a loop of bandage tight around my throbbing ankle. "Are you always such a flirt?"

He secured the bandage end and patted my knee. "Only around pretty boys who need distraction. How does that feel?"

I wiggled my toes experimentally, sending sharp twinges up my calf. I had to admit the damned thing felt better wrapped up. "Thanks." I considered my mangled bicycle. "Can I leave that here for a while? I'll catch the bus and get someone to help me pick it up later."

Pete put his hands on his thighs and pressed himself up. "No way. Doc Stella buys at least twenty dollars of produce from me every week. If she says you need to stay off your feet, that's exactly what you're going to do. I can't afford to piss her off." He looked at his watch. "We've got a few more hours until closing. I'll drive you home then." His gaze settled on mine. "You got someone to make you chicken soup once you're there?"

I blinked, trying to picture Jack making soup. Not that it mattered. With the legislature not in session, Jack wasn't around much. He'd be up in Eagle River, and Mrs. Jack would be making the soup. But not for me. I cleared my throat. "There's always takeout."

He flipped open his phone. "Hi, Sis. You know that old set of crutches? Can you bring those when you come? I think they're in the barn." He paused and glanced toward the booth. "No, he's fine. A friend sprained his ankle." He laughed and rolled his eyes. "None of your business. Just bring the crutches, okay?" Snapping the phone shut, he smiled at me. "We need to make sure you can get to the door when the pizza man comes."

"Uncle Pete?" Logan gestured toward the line forming in front of the booth. He sounded impatient.

"Coming." Pete held up his hand like he was staying a dog. "Don't move."

I eyed my pack full of photocopied articles. As pleasant as it was to sit in the sun, there really was no excuse for avoiding my research. I nodded. "I'll stay put, but would you please toss me my bag? I've got reading to do."

Or to pretend to do. The morning wore on, and I found myself distracted from the dry nineteenth-century prose of the paper I was trying to read. Debates in the 1787 New York Convention about adoption of the Federal Constitution couldn't compete with the sights, sounds, and smells of a very present, crowded farmers' market. And like with anything else, the insider experience, in this case the event from behind the booth, was totally different, and I found it completely engross-ing. Customers traded recipes with Pete, talked with Logan about school and commented on the vegetables, asked when tomatoes would be in season, discussed the weather, and gos-siped about other booths. My ankle got another icing, and with gritted teeth, I tried to write the alphabet with my toes. Only got to E. Toward the end of the morning, other vendors began showing up, trading a loaf of bread, a pie, some cinna-mon rolls, or a slab of cheese for peas, potatoes, and berries.

A tall, red-faced man stopped to buy three large bun-dles of flowers. He and Pete chatted for a few minutes about weather predictions for the next week.

As he walked away, Pete shook his head. "I'm betting the flowers won't be enough to win her forgiveness."

I stared after the man, who was pressing his way through the crowd. "Do you know him?"

He shrugged. "It's late Saturday morning. He still smells like booze, and he's buying an armload of flowers. She's probably home crying, or packing."

"And you got all that from a two-minute encounter?"

He reached under the booth and brought out the bak-ery sack of cheese empanadas he'd procured in exchange for veggies. He handed one to Logan, one to me, and bit into a third. "You'd be surprised how much you can get from first impressions." He leaned a hip against his produce table and contemplated me. "For example, you're a student at the university. Given what you said about insurance, you're probably a graduate teaching or research assistant. History?"

I fluffed the sheaf of papers in my lap. "Elementary, my dear Sherlock."

Pete laughed and stuffed the rest of the empanada into his mouth. When he could talk again, he held my gaze. "There isn't anyone you'd call for chicken soup, but somehow I don't think that's the whole story."

I looked away, the fun suddenly out of the game. I gestured toward the sidewalk where a woman fingered a basket of peas while Logan weighed potatoes for an older man in a jogging suit. "You've got a customer."

Pete arched one eyebrow and moved to help the woman. When he turned back to me, I made sure my nose was buried in eighteenth-century politics.

Fields of Gold by Dev Bentham from Love is a Light Press

find it at Amazon and Barnes and Noble.

www.DevBentham.com

Dev Bentham

Dev Bentham writes soulful m/m romance. Her characters are flawed and damaged adult men who may not even know what they are missing, but whose lives are transformed by true love.

Love is a Light Titles by Dev Bentham

August Ice

✶ ✶ ✶ ✶

The TARNISHED SOULS Series
Learning from Isaac
Fields of Gold

Coming soon to Love is a Light:
Sacred Hearts
Bread, Salt and Wine

Other books by Dev
Driving into the Sun
Nobody's Home
Painting in the Rain
Moving in Rhythm

www.ingramcontent.com/pod-product-compliance
Lightning Source LLC
Chambersburg PA
CBHW021043130626
46552CB00005B/1985